An Excerpt from…

Cupid's Corner

Heads turned as the dozen or so gathered in the room looked to Jenny, awaiting her retort. The sight reminded her of kittens watching a Ping-Pong match.

"A lot of people really want to get married, Mr. Avery." It sounded like a weak defense, even to her own ears. "That is, most people still believe in that forever-and-ever commitment. They want to take those vows and…and…well, don't you?"

He narrowed his eyes at her. "Don't I what?"

"Want to get married?"

"Why, Mayor Fox! This is all so sudden." He let out a tension-relieving laugh. Others around him joined in. "I didn't even know you cared, and now to receive this public proposal…"

Jenny stiffened. Her cheeks burned and her throat constricted. Tipping her head back just enough to appear above all the silliness, she touched the hairbow at the back of her neck and sighed. "What I propose, Mr. Avery—the only thing I am proposing, mind you—is that we get on with this meeting."

Our **Giggle** Guarantee

We're so sure our books will make you smile,
giggle, or laugh out loud that we're putting
our "giggle guarantee" behind each one. If this
book fails to tickle your funny bone, return it
to your local bookstore and exchange it for
another in our romantic comedy line.

Romantic Comedies from WaterBrook Press

SUZY PIZZUTI
Say Uncle...and Aunt
Raising Cain...and His Sisters

SHARI MACDONALD
Love on the Run
A Match Made in Heaven
The Perfect Wife

BARBARA JEAN HICKS
An Unlikely Prince
All That Glitters
A Perfect Stranger (Spring 2000)

ANNIE JONES
The Double Heart Diner
Cupid's Corner
Lost Romance Ranch (Summer 2000)

Cupid's Corner

Cupid's Corner

ANNIE JONES

WATERBROOK
PRESS

CUPID'S CORNER
PUBLISHED BY WATERBROOK PRESS
5446 North Academy Boulevard, Suite 200
Colorado Springs, Colorado 80918
A division of Random House, Inc.

The characters and events in this book are fictional, and any resemblance
to actual persons or events is coincidental.

ISBN 1-57856-134-5

Jones, Annie, 1957–
      Cupid's corner : a romantic comedy from the roadsides of Route 66
/ Annie Jones. — 1st ed.
         p.   cm.
    ISBN 1-57856-134-5
    I. Title.
    PS3560.045744C87 1999
    813'.54—dc21   99-33691
                                              CIP

Printed in the United States of America
1999—First Edition

10 9 8 7 6 5 4 3 2 1

If wedding plans have got you draggin'—

———

Costs arisin', in–laws naggin'—

———

Pack your bags, don't be a dope—

———

Grab your bride and just elope—

———

If she hollers, give her a kiss—

———

And cart her off to wedded bliss—

———

Hurry now, you're on your way—

———

To Hitchin' City USA!

———

Cupid's Corner, Kansas
The Elopement Capital of Route 66

—road signs enticing couples
to take their vows in Cupid's Corner
circa 1951

Introduction

Welcome to Cupid's Corner, Kansas, a town that exists only in this writer's fanciful imagination but typifies the romance, nostalgia, and whimsy so often attached to the real towns and attractions that once did and still do populate Route 66, the Mother Road.

While you will see some references to real places found on the old road, this place and the characters who populate it are fiction. It is my goal to allow the fantasy setting and characters to enhance and complement the real people and places found on the few miles of Route 66 that jog across the southeast corner of Kansas. There is, to my knowledge, no town holding a record for the most marriages between the Fourth of July and Labor Day, no special laws regarding marriage licenses in any one Kansas city. (I did my research and found that certain cities and counties in other states do have the right to issue immediate marriage licenses, while the rest of the state must adhere to that state's regulations regarding waiting periods.) Still, the possibility that such a place with such a history could exist sure does add a spark of fun to the proceedings, doesn't it?

I hope you enjoy your visit here in my little invented corner of Route 66 and that you come back often to visit and read book one in the Route 66 series, *The Double Heart Diner.* These are all fictitious places too, at least until you read the stories and get to know the characters. Then, I hope, you may feel they are "real" in your imagination and populated by old friends who are finding their happily-ever-afters somewhere along the remnants of old Route 66.

You are cordially invited
to the wedding of
Jennifer Kaye Fox
and
Alex Stephen Michaels
at Cupid's Corner Methodist Church
Two o'clock in the afternoon
The second of July...

Prologue

June 25

H ere comes the bride, all dressed in…"
"Never mind what I'm dressed in!" Jenny Fox held up her hand. The long ribbons of crisp white bathroom tissue intricately wound around her entire body in a simulated wedding gown rustled as she shook with quiet laughter. Streamers of the cheapest grade of coarse paper, fashioned into a veil and clamped to her head with half a dozen bobby pins, trembled around her shoulders. "Would somebody just take the picture so I can out of this getup? The games are over. Let's get on to the good stuff!"

"And those, my friends, are the very first words our bride will say to her husband after saying 'I do.'" Jenny's sister, Bobbie Ann Fox-Mayfield, waved one hand in the air with a flourish to signal that the games at the bridal shower had concluded. "Punch and cake in the dining room, everybody! Then Jenny can open her gifts and realize what good taste we all have despite the fact that we've all grown up and live in what the groom-to-be considers a one-horse town without the horse."

Jenny winced to hear again her fiancé's running joke about the small town of Cupid's Corner, Kansas. Alex

1

Michaels had been born here, just as she had. He'd grown up in a cottage house one street over from the two-story colonial she was now standing in, the very house the two of them would soon occupy as husband and wife after they bought it from her parents.

Jenny wrapped her arms around her chest, crushing the hastily draped paper that looped around her neck and encircled her waist. Try as she could to picture herself and Alex Michaels living in this house, the image simply would not come into focus for her. Celebrating holidays, raising a family, having Sunday dinners after church, growing old together here—none of the things she associated with her future in Cupid's Corner came clearly to mind. That scared her a little. A bride—even one in a tacky paper dress—should have those kinds of warm, wonderful thoughts, shouldn't she?

Jenny chewed at her lower lip and tried to push down the anxiety rising in her chest. Pre-wedding jitters. That's what her mother had called it when Jenny had tried to tell her she was having second thoughts. Not that she didn't love Alex—she did—but she just couldn't help but wonder how two people with such different hopes and dreams could be happy together forever, especially if it meant one of them would have to give up those dreams.

Alex had always spoken of wanting out of the small-town lifestyle, of moving away to try the excitement of a big city. Jenny struggled to convince herself every day that this phase of his life had passed—that his years away at college and then med school had satisfied that restless longing to live elsewhere, and that he was ready to settle down.

She'd certainly had her fill of life outside the haven of her hometown when she'd gone away to finish her education. After graduating from Kansas State University two years ago, she couldn't wait to get back to the people, the places, the values she held so dear. And she'd brought with her a renewed enthusiasm to preserve everything that made this town special. She would use that enthusiasm and more at her new job working for the chamber of commerce.

Who was she kidding? She pretty much *was* the chamber of commerce. It had taken her two years of letter writing and campaigning, but she'd finally convinced the town council to hire someone to head the chamber on a paid basis, allowing that person to give the task their all. And Jenny was that person. It was not a responsibility she took lightly. The floundering town's prosperity might now well rest on her ability to represent and market the town well.

She smiled to herself and twirled one strand of long, curly dark hair around her finger, biting her lip to still the flutter of anticipation in her stomach. At last, she could give back to Cupid's Corner some of what it had given her.

"Look at her, lost in a daydream. I bet I can guess about what…or should I say about who? Or is it whom?" Jenny's mother put one hand on Bobbie Ann's back to nudge her toward Jenny.

"Oh, we all know what she's thinking about." Bobbie Ann moved to stand next to her sister. "About the day she wears her real gown and becomes Mrs. Alex Michaels."

Jenny sputtered something unintelligible and let it go. How did you explain to the women who had done so much to put together a huge wedding that you were more focused on your new job than your new husband?

Jenny's mom didn't give her the chance to explain anything anyway, as she gestured broadly, waved a disposable camera in the air, and cried out, "Now, big smiles, girls. Think about those gorgeous, successful men of yours and say 'diamonds and emeralds and rubies'!"

Bobbie Ann gritted her teeth and obliged. "Diamonds and emeralds and rubies."

"Oh my!" Jenny tossed in.

"Jenny!" Mom clucked her tongue as she lowered the brightly colored camera from her eye. "How can I take a picture if you're going to clown around like that?"

"Mom, I'm dressed in a—" She broke off, looked at Bobbie Ann, and sighed with good humor. "Oh, never mind."

Their mom did not get her reputation for being ditsy without cause. Still, she was a good woman and one terrific mom, and Jenny knew the joke about the jewels had been just that, a joke. Mom had never encouraged them to seek material wealth in a mate but to marry for love—hopefully to upstanding, churchgoing men.

Alex was both, or at least he had been. Though his schedule had affected his church attendance these last few years, Jenny assured herself that he'd get back into the routine again after their marriage. She felt the Lord must surely understand about doctors missing church services, especially when they worked so hard to help as many people as possible, as Alex would soon be doing.

As a doctor, Alex could play a big role in sustaining the independence and viability of their community. With some not-so-subtle nudging by Jenny, Alex had admitted he could serve his residency under old Doc Hobbs at what had once been the county hospital but was now really more of an all-purpose clinic and emergency-care facility. That situation would suit Alex perfectly since he had specialized in emergency medicine, and Jenny believed it would give Alex a chance to get reacquainted with the slower pace of life here. Then eventually he could take over the clinic for the older doctor, who had been his mentor and, even more, like a grandfather to Alex.

It all seemed so perfect, perfect for Doc, perfect for the town, perfect for...well, everyone. Didn't it? Jenny clenched her fist, wadding bits of her "gown" into her damp palm.

"Now, stand together, girls, and smile."

Just the sound of her mother's sweet voice assuaged the tension building in Jenny. Jenny wondered what she was worried about. Once Alex returned to live in Cupid's Corner in two weeks—after their wedding next week and the honeymoon to end all honeymoons—he would love the life here as much as she did. This town that Jenny cherished, that held her hopes for the future as well as her fondest memories of the past, would become their home forever.

A blinding flash startled her out of her reverie.

"Isn't that just precious?" Jenny's mom raised the tiny camera like a spokesmodel, so that Jenny wasn't sure if her sometimes flighty mother meant to compliment the picture, the paper gown, or the product. "Now stand still, girls. Bobbie Ann, move in closer to your little sister, and for goodness' sake, smile! I want to take another photo in case the first one doesn't turn out. This is a picture Daddy and I will want to take with us to Arizona."

The mention of her parents' impending departure from Cupid's Corner struck a sad chord in Jenny's heart, but she knew that her father's health, which had been poor for nearly two decades, demanded the change. Both he and her mother would have a better quality of life in their retirement condo, while Jenny remained here, intent on improving the quality of life for everyone in this town.

"Smile, Jenny. Smile. This is a landmark occasion, you know. My two girls, one about to be a bride, the other about to be a mommy for the first time!"

"Mom!" Bobbie Ann's face went beet red.

"Oh! I wasn't supposed to tell yet, was I? Well, surprise!"

The flash went off to underscore Mom's words despite the fact that she had the camera pointed at the carpet.

"No kidding, surprise!" Jenny's heart leapt with sheer joy at the news her mother had gushed out, obviously without Bobbie Ann's consent. She turned to her sister, suspecting her eyes might just bug right out of her head as she asked, "Is that true? You're…you're…"

"Yes." Bobbie Ann's face radiated happiness from her sparkling green eyes to her high, round cheeks and easy smile.

Everyone said the two girls looked like twins in their faces but like two strangers in their builds, as Jenny was long-limbed and lean while Bobbie Ann was a few inches shorter and nicely padded, as Bobbie Ann's husband, Mark, liked to say. Nicely padded and about to get more so, Jenny suddenly realized.

She threw her arms around her sister for a big hug, and as their mother's camera flashed again, Jenny whispered, "When did you find out? How far along are you? Why didn't you tell me?"

"I didn't want to detract any from your big celebration, so I've kept it a secret for a few weeks. I planned to make the announcement after the wedding." Tears bathed Bobbie Ann's eyes, and she sniffled.

Jenny felt her own emotions begin to swell. She reached up and tore off a length of the white paper still adorning her head and body and handed it to Bobbie Ann. "I know you two have been praying about having a baby for a long time now."

"Yes, we have. And I think more than half the town has been praying right along with us." Bobbie Ann dabbed the tissue at the dampness on her cheek.

"That's one reason I love this place so much—people are

willing to do whatever they can for others." Jenny blew her nose on a scrap of what had been her pretend wedding gown. "All these years that Daddy has been sick, they always did so much to help us out."

"Speaking of helping out, I'm going to have to count on you more than ever now, with Mom and Daddy leaving. And Mark's promotion to regional manager means he'll travel a lot, and—"

"Say no more." She took Bobbie Ann's hand. "I'll be here for you. And for the baby. I'm not going anywhere, I promise."

This time Bobbie Ann yanked free a strip of tissue to blot her eyes. "Thank you so much, Jenny. I knew I could depend on you. Everyone always knows they can depend on you, Jenny. That's why the town placed its trust in you with that new job. You won't let them, or me, down for anything."

A hard lump filled Jenny's chest at that tall order, but she did not let her expression show any doubt or concern. The two of them simply stood there for a moment, crying softly and pulling off pieces of the tissue bridal ensemble as the need arose.

"Now, no tears, you two. This is the happiest time of our lives, you know." Mom gave them each a hug and planted pink lipstick-smeared kisses on their cheeks. Then she straightened away, holding up the camera. "Got to get some pictures of the cake before Aunt Maddie demolishes it trying to cut out the piece with the most sugar roses on it."

Bobbie Ann and Jenny both laughed.

Mom hurried off.

Jenny began to follow when Bobbie Ann caught her by the hand and pulled her back. "She's right, you know. This is the happiest time of our lives, so far. Just like we used to dream. Our lives are turning out perfectly in every way."

"Yeah, perfectly." For one heartbeat, Jenny thought of hugging her sister tight and pouring out all her doubts and reservations. But Bobbie Ann's condition and the promise Jenny had just made to always be the one her sister could rely on stopped her cold. She managed a smile, cleared her throat to chase away any lingering weakness in her voice, and said, "Everything is going to be all right for both of us, Bobbie Ann. Everything is going to be perfect."

"Jenny, are you sure you're all right? You look a little—I don't know—worried, unsure. Are you having second thoughts?"

Jenny bit her lip to keep from suddenly unburdening her reservations on her pregnant sister. Jenny loved Alex and trusted in God to make their union strong; that was enough to make it all work out, wasn't it? It had to be enough. She opened her mouth to reassure Bobbie Ann that all was well when the doorbell cut her off.

"Who could that be?" Bobbie Ann's tone rang with quiet irritation at the interruption. "Everyone we know is already here."

"Probably a delivery." Jenny pounced on the opportunity to get away, clear her thoughts, and put herself back in a better frame of mind. She gave a carefree smile. "We've been getting them all week from Alex's med-school friends."

"Ooh, then you'd better go see what it is." Bobbie Ann must have bought Jenny's relaxed act, because she gave her sister a hug and joked, "Coming from the doctor type, it could be something good."

"Ha! These folks aren't getting doctors' salaries yet. More than likely it's something they got a discount on through the school. One of them actually tried to pass off a petri dish as an ashtray."

"What doctor would give you an ashtray?"

"One that couldn't think of any better disguise for a petri dish, of course." Jenny headed toward the door, seizing the chance to get away from the party and pull herself together.

She strode purposefully down the hallway, her dress swishing around her ankles as it began to sag and droop in the places where she and Bobbie Ann had helped themselves to bits and pieces. Jenny thought about pulling the whole thing off before she opened the door, but with the veil pinned on tighter than an old maid clinging to the bridal bouquet, she decided against it. Explaining the big picture—the shower, the game, the photo—seemed infinitely easier than trying to relate to a total stranger why she had toilet paper bobby-pinned to her head, she quickly decided.

The bell rang again.

"I'm coming, I'm coming, hold your horses, would—" She swung open the door to find Alex on her doorstep. Her heart leapt, not from wild, romantic love, but from the clash of emotions created by her anxiety over the marriage and her fiancé's sudden appearance.

"How can I hold my horses, Jen? This is strictly a one-horse town, you know, without the—"

"One horse," she filled in for him without missing a beat. She blinked to let her eyes adjust to the bright summer sunlight that seemed to turn Alex's sandy hair to a lustrous gold and bounced off the glaring white of his shirt as it stretched over his broad shoulders.

"Nice dress. Did you get it off the rack or off the roll?" His mouth lifted into the kind of smile that usually made Jenny's knees wobble.

This time her entire body reacted, tensing and stiffening as though bracing to take a blow.

"Why are you here, Alex?" she said so softly it hardly stirred the wisp of tissue that lay against her cheek. Had he come to tell her he'd been suffering the same confusion she now felt? Did he also wonder if they could really make their vows last a lifetime despite their many differences? She wanted to know, but then again, she did not want to know. She wet her lips. "You weren't supposed to get into town for two more days. What's wrong?"

"Why does something have to be wrong? Couldn't I just have wanted to see the prettiest girl to ever wear a designer wedding gown by Charmin?" He crooked his finger beneath her chin. "Nothing is wrong, Jenny. In fact, things could not be more right. I have some exciting news to tell you, and it just couldn't wait another minute because it's going to mean some big changes."

"Changes?" she murmured. She did not like the sound of that. A cold sense of dread gripped deep in the pit of her stomach. The one thing she had hung her hopes on, the one thing she had let herself believe would ultimately allow it all to work out was that things would go exactly according to her plans. *No changes*. "Alex, what are telling me?"

"I applied to do my residency at one of the best hospitals in Kansas City—"

"You never told me. When did you do that?"

"Awhile back, before we got engaged." He dashed it off as if it excused his hiding from her this piece of life-altering information. "When I applied doesn't matter anyway, Jenny; it's when they want me to start that's so exciting. Next week. Can I come in so we can talk about this? We've got a lot of things to deal with and not much time if we hope to be moving to Kansas City right after the wedding."

"No." The word sounded as quietly stunned as she felt.

"No, what? No, I can't come in? I saw all the cars out there and remembered it was your shower, but since I'd come all the way to the corner of nowhere I—"

"No." She said it this time with more conviction.

"No? No to what? Jenny, you're not making any sense!"

"No, you can't come in. No, you can't just change everything like this. No, we cannot move to Kansas City right after the wedding. No. No. No."

He clenched his jaw. "Jenny, be reasonable."

"No," she whispered. "You kept this a secret from me, led me to believe that you were content with my plans for us when all along…" She had to swallow hard to choke back the bitterness rising in her throat. The reality of what was happening began to sink in, and a dull ache began to throb in her heart. Her world was falling apart on her own doorstep while she stood and watched in a toilet-paper wedding dress. It almost made her want to laugh out loud. Almost.

Instead she asked Alex Michaels to leave, told him that she would see to the details of calling off the wedding. He tried to protest but not too hard.

Moments later, when he climbed into his shiny new sports car, he turned and called back to her, "Jenny, are you absolutely sure this is something you won't regret later?"

All she could do was lift her hand to wave good-bye to send him on his way and whisper to herself the answer to his question: "No."

The honor of your presence
is requested
at the kickoff for a
record–breaking event!
Cupid's Corner's Wed–A–Thon
to reclaim the old Route 66 title of
Hitchin' City, USA.
66 Weddings in 58 days.
The countdown begins with the usual
Fourth of July festivities,
the parade, food booths, games, and
fireworks downtown,
and wedding number one.
See you there!

—flier posted in store windows
around Cupid's Corner

One

June 19
Two years later

"No doubt about it. Do I have some exciting news for you." Jenny felt like a carnival barker trying to stir an openly listless, skeptical, and distracted crowd into a frenzy of anticipation. Only this crowd was not some collection of disinterested passersby but her own town council, gathered to share their reports on the biggest publicity push they had ever undertaken.

She glanced at the council members and committee heads staring at her from around the oblong oak table in City Hall's narrow, musty conference room. Every pair of eyes in the cramped place were trained on her with an intensity that made Jenny feel as though she had one of those red laser pointers focused on her forehead.

Everyone sat silently, waiting for Mayor Fox to tell them the news. Doc Hobbs coughed and sounded every one of his seventy-two years. He was a frequent guest at meetings, coming to show his support despite the fact that he had been under the weather of late. The town's newest resident, Joe Avery, who at twenty-nine was the youngest person in attendance—except for Jenny herself—tapped a red pen on the small page of a tattered spiral notebook.

Fine dust danced and sparkled in the late morning sun streaming in through high windows. The warm light off the yellowed paint on the plaster walls cast half the group in sallow reflection and threw shadows across the features of the rest. Consequently, familiar faces seemed far more dour and disapproving than they would ever appear in plain daylight. Joe Avery alone escaped the eerie effect in his seat at the far end of the table, directly opposite Jenny's. But then, when it came to Jenny and her ideas, Joe already had a way of looking dubious about whatever she proposed.

Jenny's pulse picked up as she scanned the room again. Was she wrong to blame the poor lighting for the grim faces around her? She couldn't be wrong, she thought. Yet she couldn't remember seeing this crowd looking so sour faced since the morning after someone served questionable chicken salad at the Memorial Day picnic a few weeks ago.

Joe had had a field day with that story. Done in the name of humor, yes, but with enough truth in the mix to make people question how well-equipped the town was to pull off the event they'd undertaken. Jenny herself had wondered then if that fiasco was an unsavory foretaste of the summer to come. Her stomach knotted again, though this time sheer nerves were responsible. To counteract her apprehension, she put on an act of forced cheerfulness, smiling and trying to keep her attitude visibly upbeat. "As I said, I have some really exciting news for everyone today."

"Your news had better be more than exciting." Cavalier challenge tinged Joe Avery's soft-spoken but hard-edged voice. He leaned back in his chair, his black hair gleaming in what seemed to be the only shaft of good lighting in the room. He laced his large hands behind his head. His dark eyes glittered with fun. He grinned, and his teeth flashed white against his olive complexion. "To light a fire big enough to save this sleepy little town, your news had better be downright volcanic."

Jenny tensed, feeling her smile freeze into a tight mask, aimed in Joe's general direction. She understood that as the editor of the *Cupid's Corner Weekly News Arrow*—or the *Arrow* as it was called for short—Joe needed to take all such proclamations with a grain of salt. But she did sometimes wonder if the town and the paper wouldn't benefit greatly if Joe would go on a low-sodium diet.

"Funny, Joe. But a volcano? In Kansas?" She shook her head and gave a playful *tsk-tsk*, relying on the old proverb that a soft answer turns away wrath. She was going to get through this meeting, and through the rest of the summer, with poise and productivity. "We don't dare even consider it. A volcano would turn the entire state into the world's largest hot-air popcorn popper!"

The crowd chuckled quietly. Jenny didn't know if that was out of amusement, politeness, discomfort, or just a show of support by others who found Joe a little too outspoken for a newcomer to an old way of life.

"The World's Largest Hot-Air Popcorn Popper." Joe swept one open hand out before them as if reading a banner.

Jenny had never noticed before how strong Joe's hands were—long, blunt fingers with neatly trimmed nails but callused from holding something other than a pencil. She wondered what else she had never bothered to notice about this man—what she had chosen to ignore because she could not look past their political and ideological differences.

Where Jenny wanted uplifting portrayals of small-town life in the paper, Joe thought that only through exposing their problems could they overcome them. Jenny hoped to shine a spotlight on the positive, like a guiding beacon. Joe considered his harshest editorials akin to flipping on the kitchen light late at night to catch all the cockroaches that flourished in the darkness.

"Now *there's* a tourism draw people would really be interested in." Joe chuckled, as always lacing his biting opinion with his more mellow and genuine good humor.

Jenny blinked, scrambling to get her thoughts back on track and banish the image of bugs scattering beneath the fridge.

"Cupid's Corner: Volcanic Popcorn Capital of the World." Joe stroked his chin. Whether he knew it or not, the gesture emphasized the hint of a dimple on one of his cheeks. "Now, that's a concept a guy can *sell!* 'See the hourly eruptions of sweet Kansas Korn'—spelled with a *K*, of course. 'Learn the mysteries of the underground butter vats and tour the—'"

Dimple or no dimple, editor or egomaniac, he was spouting nonsense, and Jenny had to put a stop to it. She clenched her teeth, a fairly common tendency in her communications with the infuriating know-it-all. "Do you have a point with all this, Mr. Avery?"

"Yes, Mayor Fox, I do." He leaned forward, bracing his forearms against the edge of the table. He dipped his chin and riveted his cool gaze on her, creating the picture of a dispassionate journalist. Yet his shirt sleeves, which he'd rolled up to his elbows as if ready to get down to work, strained against his biceps. His angular jaw tightened just enough to give away the depths of his underlying annoyance. "My point is that to create a viable tourist attraction, one has to offer something that—for whatever reason, curiosity, relaxation, or basic need—draws people to it. Lots of people."

"That's what I believe we have done with our record-setting summer idea, Mr. Avery."

"Ha." He said it just like that too, not as a burst of laughter but more as an out-and-out calling her on the carpet. "Sixty-six weddings in fifty-eight days? That's not a tourist attraction, that's a publicity stunt."

"Publicity means tourists," she countered.

"A few, maybe, and some press coverage. That's good, I suppose. But for a town with the kinds of problems we have here, it's like putting a Band-Aid on a broken arm."

"And if you had your way, what would you have me do? Bury the patient for a hangnail?"

"I'd have you take into account that what this town needs is something that not only capitalizes on the Route 66 nostalgia connection but also gets people into our town spending money and stimulating our economy. In order to do that you've got to give people something they really want."

Heads turned as the dozen or so gathered in the room looked to Jenny, awaiting her retort. The sight reminded her of kittens watching a Ping-Pong match.

"A lot of people really want to get married, Mr. Avery." It sounded like a weak defense, even to her own ears. "That is, most people still believe in that forever-and-ever commitment. They want to take those vows and…and…well, don't you?"

He narrowed his eyes at her. "Don't I what?"

"Want to get married?"

"Why, Mayor Fox! This is all so sudden." He let out a tension-relieving laugh. Others around him joined in. "I didn't even know you cared, and now to receive this public proposal…"

Jenny stiffened. Her cheeks burned and her throat constricted. Tipping her head back just enough to appear above all the silliness, she touched the hairbow at the back of her neck and sighed. "What I propose, Mr. Avery—the only thing I am proposing, mind you—is that we get on with this meeting."

It certainly didn't help her embarrassment that Joe Avery had asked her time and again to go out with him since he took the newspaper job six months ago—and she'd refused. She'd refused the very first time and she'd refused the very last—which was just five minutes before this meeting had started.

Even as they stood in the hallway waiting for the others to arrive, Joe had tried to get her to admit that she was still pining over, in his words, "the man that got away." That's why he believed she would not go out with the "tall, dark, and humble" editor—also his words. Well, he was tall, all right, and he did have the kind of eyes that promise both mischief and mystery, and jet-black wavy hair. As for the last part?

Jenny glanced over at the man with his chair tipped back on two legs. If Jenny were the kind to talk behind someone's back, she'd have twisted the editor's words to a more apt description—like tall, dark, and *irk*some. That's certainly the reaction he inspired in her. That and a little irritation at his insistence that she'd never really gotten over Alex.

Alex. Until six months ago when Joe, in his misplaced quest to win her affection, had begun to make such an issue of her ex-fiancé, Jenny hadn't thought about Alex in…

She couldn't lie; she thought about Alex and what might have been all the time, even now. Every event that marked the passing of time in the small town—the harvest dance, the Christmas choir, the homecoming parade—only emphasized to Jenny how much she wished she had someone to share it with, someone who could appreciate it as much as she did.

She blinked and in that instant realized that tears bathed her eyes. The room had fallen utterly silent, everyone waiting for her to say or do something. She sniffled and blinked again, feeling heat rise in her cheeks at her silly lapse into sentimentality.

It was the pressure, she decided, that had her so emotionally vulnerable. The pressure to do well, to help those who were counting on her now, to reach her goal of the best publicity and tourism event this town had ever seen.

She threw back her shoulders, angled up her chin, and tapped her small gavel on the oval block of wood resting beside a haphazard pile of papers. "As the mayor of Cupid's Corner, it's my job, among other things, to keep things orderly and efficient in these meetings. I apologize if I let myself get distracted from that obligation. We have a lot to get accomplished and less than two weeks to get everything in place. Shall we proceed?"

Mumbled agreements answered her, but for good measure she took one last look at Joe, who frowned, dropped his chair flat on the ground with a thud, then nodded in concession.

"Now, you are the last people who need me to stand here and relate to you the illustrious history of our town." She patted the bow at the nape of her neck. She had hoped that pulling her thick brown hair back like this would make her appear more mature to these people who had watched her grow from pigtails to professional. "So, let's just focus in on the big event of the summer and the plans and publicity surrounding it. Okay?"

Again a rumble of positive answers from the group and a glare from Joe.

"Let's start with my good news." She bit her lip and held her breath for a moment. Sure, the pause helped to rebuild the tension that her brief banter with Joe and her fleeting musings over Alex had dampened, but also, Jenny needed the time to prepare herself.

She was mayor now, not just someone hired by the chamber of commerce to promote tourism in town. People relied on her. They had voted for her overwhelmingly this past fall, knowing she would do everything within her power not to let them down. And she hadn't...yet. "The good news is, we've found them."

"Found who, dear?" Doc Hobbs shifted in his seat, a concerned glint in his pale blue eyes.

"The couples!" Jenny clapped her hands together.

Silence fell so completely you could have heard a mosquito sneeze.

"You know, the *couples?*" She motioned with her hand as if encouraging them to follow her explanation. "The people we talked about? The couples we needed to come here to get married?"

"You've already found sixty-six couples to get married here?" Doc, sitting in the chair to her right, reared his head back far enough that it looked as if his clip-on bow tie might just pop right off his shirt collar. "*This* summer?"

"No, not the entire sixty-six couples, Doc!" She laughed lightly, not at him but at herself for having gotten so wound up she'd forgotten the most significant detail of her announcement. "Sorry. Some days, I don't know where my head is. We've just found the first wedding couple and possibly the last. You know, the couples who have agreed to take their vows as part of our big kickoff celebration and on the last day of the event."

She sat up so straight in her chair, she could have earned a gold star for comportment from her first-grade teacher, Miss Withers. "It wasn't easy to get a young couple willing to take their vows before an entire town of strangers. But we've done it, I think."

"The fact that you've got press coverage and some of the local merchants to promise to deliver some goodies sweetened the deal, I'm sure." A scowl replaced the lingering smirk on Joe's face.

"Thank you for reminding me, Joe." She gave him a bright smile that added a touch of "you're not going to unnerve or divert me again" to her response. "We need to be sure we all express our gratitude to Tie the Knot Menswear for supplying the grooms' clothes, to Something Borrowed for the rental supplies, and to Bouquets and Boutonnieres for the flowers. Joe, are you getting all these names down for the paper?"

"Tie the Knot," he muttered, his eyes on the crabbed writing before him. "Something Booted, Bouquets, and blah-blah-blah."

"Joe!"

"I'll print them correctly in the paper," he assured her with a grin and a wink. "But I don't mind going on record as saying that I think all these cutesy names for businesses are a bit over the top."

"Oh, that reminds me, don't forget to mention that the Cake Topper is providing the—"

"What's wrong with those names?" someone interjected from the midsection of the table.

"It's a theme," someone else chimed in. "They passed an ordinance in the forties that said all downtown business names had to follow a wedding theme."

Doc Hobbs spoke up. "We got a law passed up at the state capital a couple of years later allowing this very city hall to issue marriage licenses on the same day folks applied for them—instead of the three-day wait in other parts of Kansas."

His tone was more like that of a patient teacher than the combative manner of the others. "The town theme was a big influence in getting that done, and getting that done helped make this town the place to come if you want to elope."

"People, please. Please." Jenny rapped the gavel lightly. Joe had almost succeeded in getting them off track once again, and she was not happy about it. "The point is, I have found two of our crucial wedding couples."

"Two down, just sixty-four more to go." Joe tossed his pen down atop his open notebook like a gauntlet.

"We've gone over this before, Joe. The town already averages over forty weddings during that period without any special events or advertising anyway." Jenny clenched the handle of her gavel in her damp palm. "The record is fifty-seven weddings in fifty-eight days. We've chosen to strive for sixty-six to tie in to the Route 66 lure. That means we're only talking about an increase of twenty-some weddings. With our big publicity push, word of mouth, plus the enthusiastic cooperation of our hometown paper…" She fixed her gaze on him and, remembering her earlier commitment to the proverb of the soft answer, smiled and gave a big thumbs-up gesture. "It's doable. Definitely doable."

He said nothing in reply, just seemed to let the quiet that followed her little speech do the work of creating an awkward moment.

Jenny cleared her throat. "Of course, if any of you have friends or family, or are yourselves in the market for a wedding in the near future, nobody here would complain if you scheduled it to take place between the Fourth of July and Labor Day!"

A wave of appreciative chuckles rolled over the room.

"Speak for yourself, Mayor. You and Joe, there, are the only ones in this room that ain't already hitched," announced someone who obviously thought they were clever.

Jenny raised her gavel but couldn't bring herself to use her position to censure a council member for taking the joke she'd started to its logical conclusion. She set the gavel aside.

"Not sure I'm in the market for a marriage just yet myself," Joe said. "Haven't met the right girl—or should I say haven't gotten the right girl to meet me on some kind of common ground?" He leaned forward, his gaze locked on to hers and that irresistible hint of a smile on his lips. "But what do you say, Mayor? Do you believe in this project enough to participate yourself?"

Jenny blinked.

"Theoretically, of course," he added. "If Mr. Right were to walk in that door today, would you be willing to stage your wedding to coincide with your record-breaking effort?"

For one fleeting moment her mind went to Alex and the wedding that never was. Would she have rushed ahead with it, even with her misgivings, for the sake of her project? She didn't know, but she did have an incredible sense of relief that she was never handed that option back then. She fixed her gaze on Joe's face, his eyes seeming to pierce beneath the surface of her composed facade. She wondered if he knew she'd been thinking of "the man that got away."

She wet her lips and adjusted the bow at the back of her head. She met his steadfast gaze with one she hoped showed more wry humor than savvy political sidestepping of far too personal a question. "Mr. Avery, judging from my luck with men, if Mr. Right walked through that door today, it would be on the arm of gorgeous Mrs. Right and the two-point-five Right children. As for getting married just to help the town reach its goal—well, I pledged Cupid's Corner my service, not my sanity. The answer is—Ow!"

"So, sorry, my dear." Doc shifted in his seat, uncrossing his long legs. "Was that your shin I kicked with my big old foot?"

"Yes." And he'd done it on purpose, Jenny would bet the farm—if she owned a farm or believed in betting. She did neither, so she just sighed and turned her attention back to Joe and the firm stand she wanted to take to assure everyone she wouldn't be adding to the summer's wedding tally. "You can put it in the paper, I won't—

"So, then, you found the couple."

Jenny blinked at Doc Hobbs. "What?"

"The couple. Your news was that you'd found the couple, correct?"

"Yes, I…that was my news." She graced the older man with a tender smile, then opened her mouth to address Joe and the curious crowd again.

"Good. Just wanted to make sure I got it straight about your big news." Doc spoke a little too loudly and to no one person in particular, it appeared. "You've talked to us about so many things over these past few months, a fellow gets confused. Did you find some magazines and television stations to cover the story? Locate more Route 66 associations and devotees to help promote our project? Hunt up a treasure trove of old photographs of couples married in town for that display you wanted set up in City Hall?"

"Oh." Jenny glanced at the crowd, then at Doc, unsure if he was being difficult or really wanted answers. Either way, she quickly concluded, answering the elder citizen's questions certainly took precedence over her need to let everyone know she was off the marriage market. "I…I guess I forgot you weren't at the last meeting when I went over all those things you mentioned and then some. I apologize for not having caught you up to speed on the big doings."

"Sweetheart, at my age, the last thing a fellow worries about is speed." He folded his bony but still nimble hands on top of the new black cane he'd started using this past winter. "I just hate to be left behind in the dust!"

Jenny smiled, but in her heart she felt sadness at Doc's failing condition, and embarrassment that she had not started the meeting off by welcoming him back and asking after his health.

That was how things were done in Cupid's Corner—people first, politics later. Her eagerness to get everyone fired up over her news had marred her judgment. After all, Doc had overseen the births of perhaps half the town's population. Joe Avery's mocking attitude and his earlier inferences about her feelings for Alex had not helped either.

Jenny folded her arms over her one all-purpose business suit and tapped the toe of her blue pump. She'd let herself lose sight of the real priorities of her small town for a moment and in doing so had lost the focus of the meeting. That was no way to reach her constituency or her goals.

"No one is going to leave you in the dust, Doc." She relaxed her arms and gave him a warm, sincere nod of acknowledgment. "Nobody could. You've still got more get-up-and-go than almost anyone here."

Doc put on a good show of scanning the sampling of his friends and neighbors, then sighed and grumbled jokingly, "I'm not sure that's saying much, given I'm in the company of folks who couldn't move or think quick enough to keep their names off the ballot for town council."

Warm laughter answered him.

"But I'll take it as a compliment." Doc gave Jenny a wink.

"You'd better, or I'll see to it *your* name appears on the council ballot next year." She winked right back at him.

"No, not that!" He held up one hand.

Jenny noticed a tremor in his long fingers that she had never seen before. "How are you doing, Doc? We're all so glad to have you sitting in with us today. Does this mean you'll be back at the clinic soon?"

"I'm much better, thank you, Jenny. Glad to be here myself—glad to be anywhere, for that matter." He laughed; then the laughter abruptly turned into a cough.

Jenny leaned forward, concern for the dear man hushing her voice to a whisper. "Are you sure you should be out and about already? You need to take care of yourself."

"Now, don't go saying that out loud," Doc warned. "Nurse Pritchet hears you and she'll skin us both. You know she thinks she's the only one who can take care of me. Wouldn't trust me to take care of myself if I was my very own patient."

The group gave a knowing laugh about Doc's longtime, long-suffering nurse.

Jenny studied the man with an anxious gaze. "Well, I'm sure Nurse Pritchet would have you take your time getting better before you even think of going back to the clinic, much less these meetings."

"I have my reasons for being at this meeting." He shooed away any concern she might try to offer with a wave of his hand. "But Jenny, sweetheart, I'm not sure when or if I'm going back to the clinic."

A startled murmur created a buzz in the cramped room.

"The town losing the clinic?" Joe pressed his pen to a new sheet of paper and began scribbling. "Now *that's* definitely newsworthy."

Jenny half rose from her seat, reaching out to place her hand on the sleeve of Doc's rumpled suit coat. Even in summer, the white-haired gentleman always dressed in a dark suit, white shirt, and neat and narrow bow tie, unless he was in his clinic. In his clinic a white lab coat replaced the suit jacket, and a green stethoscope always hung around his neck. That image was as much a fixture of life in Cupid's Corner as the We-Do Weddings Chapel or the statue of a fat little cherub with his bow and arrow at the ready that stood on the lawn in front of City Hall. Now Doc was saying he might not go back to the clinic?

"Now, now. Calm down, everyone." Doc patted the air in a soothing gesture. "I didn't say anything about closing the clinic. I said I might not be going back to it, that's all. At least not for a while. I've practiced medicine in this town for almost fifty years—and never once did I take a leave of absence or even more than four days off in a row. High time I took a vacation, don't you think?"

"A vacation? Really?" Joe narrowed one eye at the older man, his pen poised over the notebook. "And just how long would this vacation be?"

"Two months. Just until the end of summer. Unless…" Doc let the word trail off, his gazed fixed in the distance for a second. He stroked his chin.

"Two months? Until the end of summer?" Jenny sank back into her chair, feeling a heavy weight settle over her. As mayor she saw potential crisis for her town in this announcement. "B-but, Doc, this comes at such a bad time. We're laying the groundwork for a lot of tourists and activities in town this summer. We need the clinic to stay open while all that's going on. What if there's an emergency? And think of your patients here. Bobbie Ann's little boy needs a doctor nearby, as do so many of our elderly citizens and, well, everybody. What if—"

"I've thought of that myself, sweetheart. But how much good will I be to folks if I'm not shipshape myself? I'll practice medicine till the day I die, but I'd rather not do anything to hasten that day along." He broke into a soft smile that sent creases rippling over his cheeks and fanning down from his crinkled eyes. "You're not asking Doc to do that, are you?"

"No! Of course not, I—" She had no way of responding to that without getting emotional. Despite the fact that she'd won her place as mayor by a landslide, there were those around who held her youth and gender against her. They just waited for situations where she might show her inexperience or let emotions sway her decisions.

But how could she not let emotions affect her now? Doc and the clinic were like the heartbeat of Cupid's Corner. If they went, she wondered how long the rest of the town could hold on. Jenny thought of her nephew, the baby Bobbie Ann and Mark had gone through so much to have, and how his health required routine doctor's visits, and she wanted to cry.

She drew in her breath and held it, her eyes never leaving the comforting sight of Doc's wrinkled face. She'd started the meeting today thinking she would wow everyone with good news and rally them for the hectic summer to come. Instead, as mayor, she needed now to make one of the most difficult concessions of her life, and to remain fair and professional as she did it.

"I know you, like most of us here, put the welfare of our town and its people ahead of personal problems and preferences, Doc. I know you would never make a decision like this lightly. I'm sure you've thought this through and chosen the course that's best for everybody—"

"You better believe I have." Doc pounded the tip of his cane on the floor. "I've come up with something that's going to be good for every last person involved, me and you included."

Joe spoke up. "And what would that be, Doc?"

For once Jenny was thankful for Joe's pushiness. He'd asked the one question she had wanted to ask in a far more direct manner than she'd have dared.

"I'm not at liberty to announce here and now exactly what—or who—will provide this little miracle cure." Doc shook his head. "However, if you'd come to the clinic around one o'clock, Joe, we'll hope to make it official."

"So will I," Jenny pledged.

"Give Mr. Avery fifteen or twenty minutes to get his story, and for me to get confirmation that it's going to pan out, dear." Doc gave the command just as he would tell a sick person to stay in bed, with a voice that left no room for argument. "Then you can act like a good politician and show up just in time for the hand shaking and picture taking."

"All right, Doc. I don't like the idea of not being first on the scene, but I'll follow doctor's orders." She smiled.

Doc chuckled, then coughed, then chuckled again.

Joe bowed his head just enough for her to see he understood her feelings and appreciated her stepping back to allow him first crack at whatever Doc had planned.

His acknowledgment made Jenny feel pleased and a little bit proud. She absolutely hated herself for feeling that way too. Over Joe Avery?

If she had time to think about that, she'd probably shudder in disgust. As it was, she had a meeting to conduct—and then she had to prepare for Doc's surprise, whatever it might be. She only hoped that it would furnish the kind of solution Doc promised; otherwise, her little town could be in big trouble.

Welcome to
Corner's Community General Hospital
Dedicated to the health and well-being
of the citizens, visitors, and guests
of Cupid's Corner, Kansas.
Mercer P. Hobbs, M.D.
General Practitioner
Please sign in at the front desk.
Deliveries and social calls come to the back door.
Emergencies ring bell.
The doctor is_____

—sign in the lobby of
Corner's Community General Hospital

Two

Joe watched Dr. Alex Michaels withdraw one perfect white business card from his wallet, flip it over, and write on it in large black block letters. When he finished, he snapped the cap back onto his pen and tucked it into his shirt pocket. Then, carefully, he propped the neat rectangular card atop the two brass hooks that Joe assumed once held a small sign to tell people whether Doc was available to see patients. Michaels stood back to admire his handiwork.

Joe did the same, though he kept watch from the corner of his eye on the clean-cut, golden-haired man standing beside him in the hospital lobby. "You sure you're a doctor?"

"Yes, of course I'm sure," the man snapped. "Why would you even ask that?"

"Because I can read your handwriting." Joe motioned to the card with a jerk of his thumb.

"Oh. I see." Michaels gave a nod, his expression blander than the noodles-and-biscuit special at the Wholly Macaroni Pasta Emporium over on Main Street.

No sense of humor, Joe made a mental note. He'd have to find another way to relate to the man if he wanted to get a first-class interview. "So, I think I may make that the headline for the story about your filling in for Doc Hobbs this summer: 'The Doctor Is In.'"

"Hmm." Michaels didn't even give Joe the courtesy of looking him in the eye when he patronized him with that non-answer.

The doctor was in, indeed. Joe made a quick study of the man in the Italian loafers and thousand-dollar suit. He pushed up his simple, all-cotton shirt sleeves, then shifted his beat-up leather athletic shoes on the dull tile floor. The doctor was in, and that doctor was none other than the man who had dumped Jenny Fox a week before their wedding—according to local gossip.

Joe felt a clenching deep in his throat, as if he needed to swallow but could not. He did not like Alex Michaels. In fact, he felt half tempted to grab the guy by the perfect knot in his blue silk tie, get right in his fake-tanned face, and tell him—

Joe tugged to loosen his own tie. He hated wearing one, but he knew that it added a needed air of professionalism. As an outsider in this small town, he needed anything that would help win people over. The new doctor would not face that kind of challenge. *He* had a history here. A history that irritated Joe right to his core. Joe shifted his taut shoulders. That's what he'd like to confront the doctor about—to take him by the tie, get straight in his face, and tell Alex Michaels that if he hurt Jenny again, he'd have Joe Avery to answer to.

Why he reacted that way to the man who looked more like an escapee from a nighttime soap opera than a small-town physician, Joe would not speculate further than to call it a journalist's gut instinct. The man had acted like a creep to someone who didn't deserve it; that put a mark against him in Joe's book. That was all. Experience warned him not to trust a guy like that.

It had nothing to do with Joe's feelings for Jenny, he told

himself. Nothing to do with the fact that, with the "man that got away" in town, Joe's chances of ever getting a date with the feisty mayor had just gone from "next to impossible" to "not in this lifetime."

Joe stuffed his hands into his jeans pockets, waiting for the man beside him to speak or walk into the office or do anything to indicate that they could begin the interview. Instead Michaels just stood there, eyeing the premises with a pained look on his face.

Joe glanced around, wondering what this doctor, used to the emergency rooms of the finest hospitals in Kansas City, was thinking about the old place.

The hospital, which even in its heyday could not have been much more than a glorified five-bed infirmary, stood like a silent testament to the passing of an old way of life. Joe scanned the single row of chrome chairs with cushions in the seventies tones of burnt orange, harvest gold, and avocado green. He considered the ragged magazines strewn across a scarred coffee table with a medicine bottle cap tacked to one leg to keep the thing from wobbling. The walls needed a fresh coat of paint, preferably something besides the circa 1960 hospital beige. The blue-gray carpet, long since worn flat and thin, should have been replaced years ago. Otherwise the small facility looked clean and smelled downright antiseptic.

Joe smiled. That had to mean Nurse Pritchet was on the premises. Nobody cleaned a room, brought order to an office, cared for the sick, or kept everyone in line like Nancy Pritchet, R.N. Pritchy, as Joe had taken to calling her, was one of the first people he had met when he moved to town. She'd rented him the apartment in the garage behind her aging white frame house, and they had immediately begun a playfully antagonistic relationship that he suspected meant the old gal really liked him, underneath her bluster and bravado.

"You know, it looks like Pritchy might be 'round and about here. Maybe we should call for her, and she can help you get settled into Doc's office—"

"I know the way to Doc's office, thank you." Michaels's shoulders jerked back, and without even a glance in Joe's direction, he strode across the creaking floor. When he reached the only door that led to the clinic's back rooms, he pushed it open with one flattened hand so that Joe could pass through first. "No need to involve Nurse Pritchet unless it's absolutely necessary."

"Little scared of her, are we?" Joe muttered as he passed into the corridor lined with doors—two opening into the examining rooms and two closed, which were the reception-ist's area/file room and Doc's office.

"Absolutely not. I have no reason to fear Nurse Pritchet." Michaels sounded firm, but he did not raise his voice enough to draw the plump nurse's attention. "I also have no desire to get her mad at me."

For the first time since Joe had walked through the door, the doctor's posture relaxed a bit and his mouth twitched into what might be a lukewarm smile. Quietly, Michaels used the toe of his expensive shoe to control the swinging door, obviously to keep it from alerting Pritchy when it fell shut.

Joe questioned the action with nothing more than his professional smirk. He didn't like the pretense, did not actu-ally feel as cocky as the practiced expression made him appear, but it had always been a good tool to him as a reporter. A questioning look, letting an awkward silence linger until the person being interviewed felt obligated to say more to fill the void, those things helped him do his job. Though he found himself using them less and less since his arrival in Cupid's Corner, Joe was pretty glad he still had some of the journalistic tricks honed in the *St. Louis Post-Dispatch* newsroom.

This trick had its intended effect on Michaels right away. "You have to realize a few things, Mr. Avery." Michaels held his hand to the door like a musician stilling the last vibrating strings of an instrument. "First, I am not taking over permanently; therefore, my authority is rather tenuous around here. I cannot afford to ruffle feathers my first few minutes in town."

Michaels moved to the door of Doc's office with as much dignity as a grown man—a professional supposedly in charge of the facility, no less—could carry off while tiptoeing. All to avoid a chance encounter with a sixty-year-old woman with silver-blue hair and droopy uniform pants. The doctor opened the door with one stealthy twist of his wrist and a nudge. He stepped across the threshold first this time, holding the door open for Joe to follow.

"Besides…" Michaels peered behind them for one last furtive check of the hallway. "Nurse Pritchet has known me all my life. You've no doubt seen the way she treats poor ol' Doc."

"Some days it's like she's a drill sergeant and he's the new recruit; others like he's a four-year-old who needs her constant guidance and supervision. And then there are the days when she gets ornery." Joe slid into one of the green imitation leather chairs in front of the desk. He chose the one without the duct-tape patch because the tape tended to roll and stick to clothing. Pritchy had given him a wonderful piece of a humorous column about salespeople who had gotten stuck to that chair and the ways they had tried to gracefully extricate themselves.

"Well, if you understand how Nurse Pritchet can behave

toward Doc, then you can probably guess how she might treat someone like me—someone she has literally watched grow up." Michaels scanned the room as he spoke, clearly fascinated by what must have been to him very familiar surroundings. "Nurse Pritchet has treated me for everything from diaper rash to drawing blood so I could get a marriage license."

Joe stiffened. He thought of asking a quick follow-up question to that remark—strike while the iron is hot—but he held back. An awful lot of folks would love to learn the young doctor's side of the whole broken engagement, but it wouldn't be fair to Michaels or to Jenny.

"Nurse Pritchet isn't going to respect me for my degree or my position, Mr. Avery. Not when she can recall seeing me in my footie jammies with the cowboys on them or the time she had to help Doc extract a french fry from my nose—don't ask."

"Were these recent events?" Joe couldn't help himself.

To his credit, Michaels huffed out a soft chuckle to that, then sat, his weight plopping down and his legs sprawling outward just enough to make him look like a gangly teen rather than a polished professional. "To honestly answer the question you asked before? I'm a little scared of the lady—a little scared about being back here in Cupid's Corner at all. I'd be a fool if I weren't."

The confession came so earnestly, without any guile or arrogance, that for one moment Joe actually felt badly that he hadn't warned Michaels away from sitting in the chair with the duct-tape pants-trap.

"Of course, all that's off the record. You can't print it. Wouldn't do to shake the town's confidence in the man they've brought in to save the day, now would it?"

Joe's moment of regret passed. He reached into his shirt

pocket to get his small notebook, opening it to an empty page with a flick of his wrist. "Then let's get to the stuff that's on the record, why don't we? We don't exactly have a lot of time to waste before—"

The three small cowbells that dangled from a cord on the front door jangled to announce that someone had entered the outer lobby of the clinic. Joe tensed. Could be the doctor had his first patient. Joe checked his watch. More likely, Jenny had just showed up fifteen minutes early. Probably had Doc on her heels and Larry Hackerman, the paper's staff photographer who fancied himself the town historian, bringing up the rear.

Joe shifted in his seat. He didn't know which he dreaded more, seeing Jenny and Alex reunited for the first time since they'd split, or not seeing it and wondering how it went. He opted for not seeing it. He wasn't jealous, of course, just not interested in someone else's personal mushy stuff.

So he rushed on, thinking that if he could just get a few quotes from Michaels, he could fill in with the background material Doc had already given him and some photos. Plus, he could get observations from Doc and Jenny later. "So let's get a few questions answered real quick before people start showing up to welcome you."

"May be too late. Sounds like the word is already out that I'm here. Small-town gossip—spreads like that." Michaels frowned and snapped his fingers. "It's one of the reasons I wanted out—everybody knowing everybody else's business. That alone wouldn't be unbearable, I suppose—not like I have anything to hide. But knowing about everyone's quirks and problems is never enough."

Nurse Pritchet's voice carried through the thin wall between Doc's office and the receptionist's area. While he could not make out her exact words, Joe clearly understood she did not think anyone could have gotten past her. Then her voice took on a scolding tone, probably getting on Doc's case for any one of a thousand things she thought she knew how to handle better than he.

Michaels sighed and shook his head. "When you live in this town, you can't go to the grocery store or take your dog for a walk without someone feeling free—no, *obligated*— they feel obligated to give you unwanted advice on what to do with your life."

"Hey, they only do that because they care." Six months ago when he'd first come to Kansas, Joe could never have imagined that he would mellow enough to dispute the doctor's point. But hearing the disdain in Michaels's voice, aimed at well-meaning folks who usually wanted the best for one another, had Joe on the defensive. "Caring about each other is part of the charm and character of this place."

"Charm? Character?" Michaels laughed. "We're still off the record here, aren't we?"

"We are until you tell me for sure we're not anymore. Which means pretty much this whole conversation is useless to the paper." But not entirely useless to Joe on a personal level. He had learned a few very interesting things already. He wasn't averse to learning a few more before he got down to official business. "Rest assured, Doctor, anything you tell me now will remain confidential, but I do expect to get some kind of information out of you for my story before I leave. Deal?"

"Of course," the man said, as though insulted at any implication otherwise. "You call this place charming, right?"

"That's the way I see it, sure."

Michaels gave a derisive snort. "I've been shopping for a new house in Kansas City. And one thing I've learned in doing that is when a Realtor uses terms like *charm and char-*

acter to describe a place, I'd better run. Charm and character are just euphemisms for broken down, older than dirt, and no longer viable in today's world. It's never the kind of place I'd want to call home, trust me."

"So, you don't consider our cozy little community your home anymore?"

"Not since my parents died a few years ago." He folded his hands in his lap. "Not that I have anything against this place. It's the scene of some of my happiest memories."

Memories that would include Jenny, no doubt. Jenny at the prom, Jenny at parties and picnics, Jenny when they'd become engaged—and on the day he broke her heart. Joe bounced the pencil in his white-knuckled grip against the still unmarked page.

"I grew up here, after all, and these people are very much a part of my personal history." He said it like some statesman waxing nostalgic about all the little people who made his success possible.

"But that doesn't make it home." Joe needed to drum the point in, to make absolutely sure that Alex Michaels had no permanent ties here—for his readers' sakes, he told himself. "You still plan on buying that house and going back to work in a hospital in Kansas City?"

"Yes, I do. I'm only here for this summer, to help out my mentor, Doc, and the people in town who have supported me so long. Oh, and for one other thing."

"Yeah?" Joe leaned forward.

"I'd have to make absolutely sure this goes no further than these four walls before I could tell you," Michaels warned.

Joe slapped his notepad closed, tucked it and his pencil in his pocket, and held up his hands in mock surrender. Normally, he might not have agreed to it. These, however, were not normal circumstances. He had been here too long without one real practical piece of information to show for it.

He wasn't foolish enough to think that he could apply his powers of persuasion to wheedle Michaels into some kind of unwitting confession or to even get him to drop a hint. If he could have accomplished that, it would only require a little legwork to discover what hidden motives the doctor might have for returning to town. But the swish of the swinging door and several pairs of quickened footsteps told him he did not have that kind of time.

If he wanted to hear this—and he did want to hear it, more than he wanted to admit—he had to act now. "Okay, Dr. Michaels. I promise not to breathe a word of it. Now, why don't you tell me—what else has brought you back to Cupid's Corner?"

"I have to know." The other man leaned closer, his voice a dispassionate whisper, as if they were discussing yesterday's lunch. "If the woman I left behind in Cupid's Corner two years ago—"

Pritchy's protests halted the footsteps just outside the waiting-room door.

Joe had to know what Michaels had in mind regarding Jenny. It was the only way Joe could protect her. He just knew it. Of course, Jenny had made it perfectly clear that she did not want to entrust herself or her feelings to Joe in any way. Still, that did not change how much Joe appreciated and admired that gritty little do-gooder of a mayor. So he urged the doctor on, hoping he could use whatever he learned to help Jenny. "You have to know if the woman you left behind—"

"Sorry, Doc." Jenny's voice from the hallway intruded on the interview. "Part of being a good mayor is knowing when to take charge. I want to know what solution you've brought in to solve all our problems, and if Joe Avery has a problem with me barging in early on his big scoop, then he can just file a formal complaint with my—" In that split second, Jenny burst through the door with Doc Hobbs right behind.

"Alex!"

"Jenny!" Michaels turned toward the intruders.

Jenny gasped. Her face paled.

Joe frowned.

Doc chuckled.

Nurse Pritchet clucked like a hen fussing over her chicks.

Alex leapt from his seat, or at least he tried to. The chair with the tricky duct tape jerked upward, attached to his flawlessly tailored trousers.

That's when Larry Hackerman insinuated himself into the scene. His camera flashed.

Everyone bellowed out their obvious objections.

Larry snapped another photo, then another.

Joe buried his head in his hands, sighed, then gave in to the moment and started to laugh. He hadn't gotten the interview. He hadn't gotten away before Jenny met with her lost love. And he had no idea why Michaels had come back to town or how it concerned Jenny.

But he did take consolation in one thing. Even in Jenny's eyes for this one moment in time, Joe figured he had to look like a better catch than a beet-faced man with a chair taped to his behind.

He decided to savor that thought while he could. Because if the look of emotional turmoil in Jenny's eyes was any indication, it might be the last thing he found amusing this whole, long, record-setting summer.

You were there when we came special delivery,
and helped us get well when the flu had us shivery,
You help keep us well, to grow strong and tall,
and bandage us up if ever we fall.
You're always so kind, always smiling, not gruff,
For all that you do, Doc,
We can't thank you enough!
From
Miss Withers's First Grade Class
1974

—framed poem with illustrations
hanging on Doc Hobbs's office wall

Three

"Doc, how could you? Bringing Alex here without even asking me or telling me or…or…"

"Warning you," Joe murmured from behind her back.

"Yes, *warning* me." Jenny's heart pounded as though she'd just outrun her greatest fear. She stared over Doc's shoulder at the closed door to his office, where even now Nurse Pritchet was helping Alex extricate himself from the notoriously sticky chair while they waited in the hall.

Jenny knew she had to calm herself, to gain some kind of distance and perspective about the terrible jolt she'd just received. She drew in a deep breath and held it, trying to focus on the smells of rubbing alcohol, disinfectant cleaners, and scorched coffee. What she smelled was the scent of fresh soap and baby shampoo on Joe Avery's skin and hair—that and the trouble brewing behind Doc's office door.

For a second, she considered elbowing the newspaper editor to make him move back a step, but she stopped herself from venting that misdirected anger. Besides, if she were totally honest, she'd admit to taking some comfort in having Joe behind her. That way if the trauma of all this were to suddenly overcome her and she fainted, he'd catch her before she hit the floor and added a concussion to her list of things gone wrong today.

Joe *would* catch her too. She had not one bit of doubt about that. After the surprise Doc and Alex had sprung on her, she might well question her judgment concerning people, especially men. But she did not doubt good ol' tall, dark, and...honorable, she mentally amended her usual description of Joe.

He'd be there for her—if only to say "I told you so" and then ask her out again.

Jenny blinked. She must be in shock. Why else would she be standing there thinking about how reliable Joe Avery was when Alex Michaels was ready to emerge any moment and announce that he'd come to stay the summer?

She swallowed hard and pinched the bow in her hair between her thumb and forefinger. "That's the very least you could have done, Doc. You could have warned me that you...that he...that this—*this*—was your solution that would be the best for everyone!"

"It *is* what's best for everyone. I get my vacation and rest. The town gets a doctor during your big summer event. And you get—"

"A headache." She put her palm over her forehead. "I am definitely getting a headache."

"Really?" Joe muttered, moving in closer so that only she could hear him. "That's an interesting response to getting a second chance with the man that got away."

A second chance? With Alex? Could it be? Now her head and her chest hurt. This was too much, happening too fast.

"Jenny, honey, I'd thought you'd be pleased." Doc rapped his cane on the floor to accentuate each word.

"We'll be out in a minute," Nurse Pritchet barked from behind the closed door, obviously assuming someone had knocked on it to hurry them along.

"I am pleased." Jenny let the last word squeeze through

her clenched smile like clothes through an old-fashioned wringer washing machine. The image suited how she felt emotionally—through the wringer and hung out to dry. She added, "If only you'd have discussed it with me first so I could give my input, or at least prepared myself to—"

"I wanted to surprise you." Doc's eyes twinkled.

"I think he's confused *surprised* with *stunned.*" Joe's breath stirred a loose strand of hair trailing down along Jenny's neck.

She shivered.

"I never thought it would upset anyone, dear. I only did what seemed best for the town. Alex was finished with his residency and had the luxury of being able to accept this job, even if it is probably just temporary."

"*Probably* just temporary?" Jenny's mind raced with all the implications of that little time bomb.

"Well, yes. Of course, being an emergency-room physician, he can always find work back in Kansas City when he needs to, *if* he needs to."

"If?" She choked on the word. What else did Doc know that she didn't? Could Alex have confided in the older man that he had become disillusioned with city life so far away from his wonderful hometown where someone—where *everyone,* she hastened to revise—loved him? "Oh, Doc, this is just too much. I can't deal with all this at once."

"Deal with what? I've already taken care of all the details. There's nothing more for you to do, dear, but wait and see what happens." Doc bounced that cane again.

"Keep your britches on!" Nurse Pritchet bellowed, then her voice dropped to a moderate holler. "Not you, Dr. Michaels."

Doc laughed. "Sounds like she's convinced him that the only way to keep from tearing those overpriced pants of his is to crawl out of them first, then let her peel them away from the tape."

They heard a muffled complaint from the office, and seconds later the door flew open.

Nurse Pritchet did not look happy.

Neither did Alex.

But the duct-taped chair was vacant, and Alex had seated himself in the large leather chair behind Doc's desk.

Alex. Jenny held her breath, feeling her cheeks singe and her head spin. She lifted her chin and skimmed a hand down her business suit, taking mental inventory to insure everything was neat and tidy.

In those fleeting seconds before she crossed the threshold and faced Alex again after…after so long, she said a swift and silent prayer for a cool head and a gracious heart. The last time she had seen this man she'd been swathed in a toilet-paper gown. Now she had been given a second chance. She quickly prayed for one small concession—that whatever happened, whatever new impression she made on Alex today, it would be carried off with grace and dignity.

She exhaled slowly, opened her eyes, and stepped through the door, motioning with one hand for Doc and Joe to join them. "Well, Alex Michaels—*Dr.* Michaels—looks like you've rated a very official group to welcome you back to Cupid's Corner."

"Jenny," he whispered her name like a parched man calling for water.

She reined in her overly romantic imagination and corrected herself—he whispered her name like a man completely chagrined at the circumstances. "That's Mayor Fox, now, if you hadn't heard. And of course you know Doc and Nurse Pritchet and Larry and…well, I guess you already met Joe, too, so—"

Nurse Pritchet brushed past Jenny, effectively cutting off the entrance with her stout little body so that no one else could follow Jenny in. "So, no need for us to stand around gawking, is there?"

Jenny spun around, panic gripping high in her throat. "But I thought everyone should come in."

"Oh, you don't want a roomful of people here while you two talk, honey." Nurse Pritchet's hand clamped down on Jenny's shoulder. "Now, you men get on out of here and leave these two be for a few minutes, so they can get themselves reacquainted."

Doc and Larry each backed up a step, but Joe stood his ground. "I can't leave yet. I haven't finished my interview."

"Yes, Joe has a job to do," Jenny protested, amazed that she could croak out anything at all. "You should let him stay. I'm sure he has a lot of questions to ask, and Larry...Larry needs to get some photos."

"All of which can wait a few minutes." The cherub-faced nurse gave Jenny a devilish grin. "I know you always want to put Cupid's Corner responsibilities ahead of anything personal, Jenny, but I think it's all right to take care of just plain Cupid's concerns first, this one time."

"Cupid?" She started to glance at Alex, to get a reading on how he reacted to the bold and disconcerting comment. Then her prayer asking that she handle things gracefully flashed through her mind. If she looked at Alex right now, she might blow that possibility altogether.

"And if not Cupid, then...well, personal concerns. No use pretending that everyone here doesn't know that you two have plenty of those."

Jenny drew up her shoulders and folded her arms in her best the-mayor-means-business pose. "Nurse Pritchet, I demand that you allow—"

Doc made a playfully exaggerated wince and shook his head as if to tell Jenny she'd crossed the line and no one could help her now.

Larry scurried backward like a spider evading a thick-soled shoe.

Joe sucked in his breath, sharp and quick like someone who'd just poured lemon juice on a paper cut. Gentle amusement, mock sympathy, and some unclear emotion shone in his eyes.

"You demand? In *my* hospital?"

Jenny stepped backward, moved more by the nurse's reputation than by any actual implied threat in her flabbergasted tone or laughing expression. "That is, I…"

"Sit." The nurse pointed downward, as if commanding a collie with an attitude of kind firmness.

Jenny stepped back again, bumping her legs against the seat of a chair, but did not obey.

Nurse Pritchet huffed, then turned her attention toward the men in the hall. "You three, off to the lobby. Doc, you need to rest yourself for a few minutes. Trying to do too much too soon, you are. Larry, you can snap off a few shots of Doc and me for my scrapbook."

Larry nodded, his few remaining strands of hair bobbing like antennae.

"Jenny, dear, you sit." One sure push downward with a hand made strong by years of typing on her faithful Remington, practical nursing, and giving countless injections to squirming children sent Jenny plummeting into the chair with a *whomp.*

The landing jarred her to her teeth but did not dull her senses enough to keep her from one instant, awful realization—she's just been deposited in the chair with the duct-

taped cushion. No matter how she felt about being alone
with Alex right now, she was stuck, literally. She'd have to
wait it out, talk with Alex long enough to appease the match-
making nurse, then ask for the others to join them. Perhaps
in the commotion of their return, she could wriggle free
without too much damage to her skirt—or her decorum.

"Joseph Avery, go!" Nurse Pritchet jerked her thumb in
the direction of the lobby. "You can get a quote from Doc for
now. I'm sure Dr. Michaels will call you all back in when he's
good and ready."

Jenny sighed. She had no choice. She'd have to be alone
with Alex. She would not have time to prepare herself for it.
As the door closed she took one last look toward the hallway,
only to find Joe's steady gaze trained on her, concern and that
strange unnamed emotion in the depths of his dark eyes.

Jenny smiled to reassure him she was fine. Still, she felt
a pang of regret that good ol' Joe wouldn't be here to catch
her if she fell.

❧   ❧

"I cannot believe you did that, Pritchy." Joe had to shorten
his stride to keep from overtaking the woman, even though
she kept a brisk pace leading the group to the lobby.

"Had to." She shrugged her round shoulders. "If those
two are going to live and work in the same community this
summer, they've got to face each other sometime."

"Yeah, but you really put Jenny at a disadvantage. Caught
off guard, thrown in a room with the man that…with her
ex-fiancé."

"You wanna take a bandage off, you do it in one quick,

clean jerk. Don't drag it out or try to make it easy by taking it in small increments. Don't give the patient time to tense up or get scared and defensive."

She pivoted on the thick pads of her nursing shoes, frowned to catch Joe pulling up short to keep from bumping into her, then reached out to take Doc's arm. As she helped the older man get settled into one of the waiting-room seats, she concluded, "That's all I did for Jenny and Alex."

"That's all?" Joe crossed his arms. "Just yanked that bandage right off."

"Metaphorically speaking, of course. You can take that picture now, Larry." She situated herself on the chair's arm next to Doc.

Larry positioned himself on one knee.

Joe slipped to one side to keep from marring the photo with his glaring expression. He clenched and unclenched his fists, his arms still laced tightly over his chest. "Just like that? You just threw Jenny in there with him."

"Fast and neat." She straightened Doc's bow tie, then licked her fingertips and slicked back the old man's thin hair, much as she might a child's. "Of course it might hurt for a moment, but when that's subsided, the worst is over and the patient can go on with the business of mending, getting stronger. Right, Doc?"

Doc batted away Pritchy's hand. "It's an old-fashioned method, but yes, I'd say it should still work."

"Big smiles, now." Larry focused the camera lens.

"In the long run, I think Jenny and Alex will thank us for this abrupt measure." Doc set his cane aside and grinned that fatherly grin that everyone in town had come to know and love. "They'll find that once the initial sting fades, they're in much better shape than they had previously suspected."

Pritchy's face beamed with pride. "That's always the way

it happens when you rip that bandage off before they can mount a protest."

"Unless, of course," Joe droned in a reflection of how unenthusiastically he embraced the plan, "you strip that bandage off a wound that's not properly healed yet. You do that and you can reopen a lot of hurt, risk all kinds of complications you may not have foreseen."

"Say *cheese!*" Larry chirped.

Pritchy's smile froze.

Doc's eyes widened.

They exchanged a look of sheer panic, and then the camera flashed.

❧   ☙

"Well, Alex." Jenny straightened her back, crossed her legs, then uncrossed them and smoothed her damp palms down the rough fabric of her skirt. After two years she and Alex were alone again, and she couldn't help but worry over how he must be looking at her.

She chewed at her lower lip, regretting that she hadn't been able to bowl the man over with a great entrance. Even now she didn't exactly have the situation under control, not with her backside most likely taped to her chair. If she hoped to restore that air of grace and dignity she desperately wanted to project, she'd have to do something quick. Maybe she could dazzle him with some witty repartee.

"Hello, Jenny." Alex notched his fingers together and leaned forward over the desk, his gaze fixed entirely on her.

"Um, hello…uh, Alex." She'd forgotten how intense and blue his eyes could seem. "Wel…come b-back."

Oh, yeah, if that display of verbal dexterity didn't dazzle him, what else could? a little voice in her head quipped. For that matter, since when had that little voice in her head taken on a decidedly Joe-like tone and attitude?

She wriggled in her seat. The tape loosened—not enough to set her free with ease, but it did relinquish some of its hold. Now if only this gripping combination of dread, anxiety, and exuberance would do the same, maybe she could get through this first meeting and make her escape so she could have some time to sort this all out. "I have to admit, Alex, this is a huge surprise, seeing you here today. The only thing more surprising is this news that you're...did I understand Doc right? *You* have volunteered to stand in as town doctor this summer?"

"Shocking, isn't it?"

"That's putting it mildly. Nobody told me a thing about this."

"Nobody knew but Doc and his nurse, and they didn't have confirmation of my decision until first thing this morning." He tapped his knuckles on the calendar pad atop the old oak desk like a man weighing his words. His shoulders lifted and he let out a hard sigh. "I didn't accept this job lightly, Jenny. You, of all people, can appreciate how difficult it was for me to take on the commitment."

"Yes, I, of *all* people, have a unique understanding of how seriously you take your commitments, Alex."

He sat there silent and still for several seconds. His eyes searched her face—for what, she could not be sure: festering anger and disappointment, or perhaps the chance of forgiveness?

Instantly, regret seized her. Her tart answer had come before she could stop herself. Now it rang harsh in her mind and left her wondering how Alex might interpret it. Would he think she still held a grudge against him? Had missed him more than she would admit and even looked on him, as Joe would describe it, as the one that got away, the one she would always pine for?

Joe? How did he get into this picture? she asked herself. When had that name, that man, begun creeping into her thoughts and affecting her judgments? She shook her head, as if to jar the unwelcome presence from her mind. She no longer cared for Alex, had not been pining away for him the last two years, no matter what Joe Avery thought. This was her chance to show him just that.

To show *Alex,* she made herself clarify, not Joe. She would now show Alex that she was over him. She could not care less what Joe thought and had no intention of showing him anything except how wrong he was about her idea for the summer's wed-a-thon.

"Jenny, I—"

"No, Alex." She held up her hand. "That was uncalled for. I was as much to blame for our breakup as you were. There, now that that's said, we can move on to the present."

"Don't you even think about it, Jenny?" A wistfulness softened his voice. "About me? About us? About what might have been, if only…"

"That's history, Alex." She chose a diversionary tactic over an outright lie. She did think of him, of course. She had been thinking of him just this morning, and playing that same "what if?" game that Alex's question implied. "There's nothing we can do about what's already gone on between us. We can only look to the future now and—"

"I am so glad to hear you say that." He stood, a broad grin breaking across his face. "Because that's just how I feel too. Finally, that was why I came back."

"What was why you—" Tension bunched the muscles between her eyebrows. She cocked her head.

Alex moved from behind the desk, more like some sleek animal on the prowl than a man on the rebound from a gentle brush-off. "Oh, I have a sense of loyalty to Doc, no question about that, and gladly chose to pitch in, in my old hometown's hour of need. But still, it was that hope that brought me back here again, Jenny."

"What hope, Alex?" She gripped the arms of the tacky chair. Her head ached, and her pulse thudded high in her chest. She heard Alex speaking, saw him closing in on her, then kneeling at her side, but could make no sense of why he did it. She had meant to show him how thoroughly she'd gotten over him, and yet these did not seem to be the actions of a man who felt "gotten over." "I don't think I understand all this, Alex. What hope are you talking about? What else besides the job brought you back to Cupid's Corner this summer?"

"You did, Jenny." He placed his hand on hers. "Just like you said, I came here to put the past in its place, to help both of us grow beyond our painful history."

"That…that sounds very healthy, Alex." Then why did the words make her feel so heartsick? She dropped her gaze and caught a glimpse of his hand on hers. The sight touched her in a way she could never have predicted, and she found herself turning her fingers to entwine with his. "That sounds like the best thing for both of us. If we're going to live in a town this size for two months, we need to let go of our past. We need to find a way to get along, to work together, to concentrate on the present."

If she had just given that speech to Joe instead of Alex, he'd have razzed her for coming off sounding too much like a politician. She smiled at that.

"You're right, Jenny. We must let go of the past and concentrate on the present. It's the only way."

Hearing the phrases repeated only reinforced how much
they came off like campaign slogans. She shut her eyes and
thanked the Lord that Nurse Pritchet had chased Joe out of
the room before he'd heard them. He'd never have let Jenny
live down a couple of pure cornball quotes like that.

Alex gave her hand a squeeze, and her attention focused
fully back on him.

"It's good we've reached an understanding then," she
said. "It's going to make things so much easier. It's not as if I
didn't already have my hands full with all the wedding and
Route 66 tie-in events. Now to know that we feel the same
way…well, it's like a burden has lifted from my shoulders,
you know?"

"I know. I know exactly what you mean." He leaned over
to kiss her cheek.

She let out a tiny gasp. Her heart leapt, not from the
thrill, but from the sheer surprise of it. People did not kiss
each other on the cheek in this little corner of Kansas unless
they were relatives or sweethearts. If anyone else had done
it—except her dad or perhaps Doc—she'd have given him a
glare so scathing that steam would have risen off his
blanched face. But she'd just reached a very tentative compromise with this man, one that would enable them both to
go about their business in this tiny town without a lot of
needless embarrassment or bother. Why do anything to
jeopardize that now?

"Listen, I know you've been in the city for a while
now." She pulled away from him and launched into her
best diplomatic mode, toothy smile and all. "And you've
probably forgotten how conservative we small-town folks
can be, so maybe I should remind you that kissing is not a

casual greeting or even a run-of-the-mill friendly gesture around here."

"I never intended it as one." He leaned in farther, his eyes half shut, a faint smile tugging at his lips just seconds before they closed over hers.

Jenny placed the heels of her hands on his broad shoulders, but she did not push him away as she probably should have.

He kissed her so lightly, without lingering, that when he moved back enough to look into her eyes again, she almost wondered if it had happened at all. "Why…why did you do that?"

He brushed a loose strand of hair back from her temple. "Just what you suggested—forgetting the past and enjoying the present."

As he leaned in for a second kiss, he murmured, "And before my work here in town is through, hopefully we'll know once and for all whether you and I have a future together."

This time she did push him away. She stood with such speed and force that the tape tore free of her skirt. The chair, which had risen with her sudden bolt, clattered back to the floor. In a heartbeat, she escaped through the office door and into the hallway.

As she stormed into the lobby, Larry dodged out of her way.

Doc and Nurse Pritchet both began speaking—asking questions, she supposed, though she could not make out the actual words, nor did she stop to try.

Joe jumped to his feet.

Alex thundered down the hallway after her. "Jenny, Jenny, come back! I didn't mean to—"

Jenny kept her focus on the doorway and the freedom that lay beyond.

"Jenny, are you all right?" Joe's voice cut through the emotional swirl that had her running out into the...

Running out into the *afternoon,* Jenny mused as she paused with her hands braced against the outer door. She couldn't even get it right about running out into the night. She had to run out into broad daylight, probably to be greeted by several of her constituents. Perhaps a curious tourist with a camera would snap her photo and sell it to some tabloid with the heading "Small Town Mayor Has Big Problems."

"What did you do to her?" Joe demanded above the buzz of everyone talking at once.

"Me? I didn't do anything," Alex's voice matched Joe's in volume and intensity. "And what's it to you anyway? You're not involved with her, are you?"

"No, but at least I voted for her for mayor, which is more than you stuck around to do."

"Stop it, you two, stop it!" Nurse Pritchet cut into the fray. "This isn't accomplishing anything."

Jenny could not have agreed more. And since accomplishing things for a town that very much needed her operating at one hundred percent during these next crucial months was her first duty, she could not let any of this nonsense interfere. So, as the bickering raged on pointlessly in the hospital lobby, she made up her mind. Not Alex or Joe or even Doc and the clinic's problems would distract her any further.

She had no idea how she would manage it, but she resolved that whatever it took, she would keep herself focused on her town's goal. Then, without so much as a good-bye or a wave over her shoulder, she lifted her head high. She slipped quietly out the door, echoing the promise she had just made to herself: "No matter what, I will do this. I will do everything I can to save my town. I will restore this place as the center of love and romance, the very epitome of the blessed covenant of marriage and fidelity." She marched off into the sunshine, her teeth clenched as she added, "And no *man* had better get in my way, or else."

Welcome Wedding Guests
and
Route 66 Enthusiasts!
Swenson/Combs Wedding—7:30
Reception Immediately Afterward
Sponsored by
Mayor Fox and the Town Council
Fireworks to Follow

—*message on the marquee outside the
We-Do Weddings Chapel*

Four

"What's with the long face, Your Honor?" Joe strolled across the lush green lawn of the We-Do Weddings Chapel, wearing a grin brighter than any blinding white sparkler.

"Don't 'Your Honor' me. You think I haven't noticed you only do that when you want to needle me?" Jenny folded her arms and tapped the toe of her lace-covered tennis shoe on the sidewalk. Around them the townsfolk gabbed and gathered, many hurrying in to get good seats for the ceremony scheduled to take place in just...

Jenny squinted over at the bank clock. The squared digital numbers glowing down over the chaos of the town's festivities made her heart beat faster. So little time and so much yet to do. She could not afford even a momentary diversion.

But since Joe had already seen her and she'd acknowledged him, she could hardly just turn and run off. She'd give him thirty seconds and no more, she decided. Two minutes, tops, then she had to get moving again. The fate of everything she'd arranged hung in the balance. "I don't have time to chat, Joe. So let's cut right to the chase. I can only suppose your calling out my official title means you've already heard about our impending fiasco."

"Fiasco?" He acted surprised, but Jenny did not believe it for one minute. Not Joe, not the newspaper editor, not with gossip this hot and its consequences for her and her event so chilling.

Jenny pushed back her natural-colored straw hat adorned with a bold silk Kansas sunflower. She swept her hand over her forehead and crinkled up her nose in reaction to the glare of the summer sun, perched low above the plains.

Joe came to a stop right beside her. He looked relaxed and a bit cocky, with his face slightly sunburned from covering the day's activities for the paper and his hair ruffled by the hot wind. Instead of his usual cotton business shirt and hastily knotted—or was it hastily loosened?—tie, today he had on blue jeans, a white T-shirt, and wide red suspenders. But his smug grin had not changed or lessened with this more casual attire.

"Well, you certainly dressed for the occasion." She crossed her arms over her pale shirt worn under a simple blue sundress.

"If by that you mean the occasion of an out-of-control, Fourth of July/Route 66 Reunion/Annual Town Celebration/Kickoff for the Record-Breaking Summer and Wedding ceremony, then, yes. Yes, I have." He hooked one thumb under a jarring red suspender strap and let the wide elastic snap back against his broad chest. "I did some research on the matter and found out that this is indeed the traditional costume of the citizenry of this corner of Kansas for just such an event."

She pursed her lips and narrowed one eye at him, telling him silently that she was in no mood to endure any wise-cracks about how backward or corny he found their town.

Totally unscathed by her blistering glare, he put two of his fingers to a spot that would have been his lapel had he been wearing a sport coat and added, "Though maybe I should have popped for one of the sunflower boutonnieres, which my extensive study of native habits—and a dandy sales pitch from the town florist—tells me are pretty popular even for plain ol' wedding guests."

She had no time for this useless banter. Obviously, he wanted to know what she knew, and he thought the best way to get that was to lull it out of her with silly chatter. She shook her head. She'd be direct. She would not lie, but neither would she stand here and unwittingly feed the man ammunition to say "I told you so"—or, worse yet, to print it in the paper—regarding the pitfalls of her summer public-relations event. "You're lucky you passed on the popping, then, aren't you, Joe?"

His black eyebrows slashed downward in a show of confusion.

"For the sunflower to wear to the wedding." Having neither the time nor the patience for this charade, she reached over to point to the place just centimeters from where his fingers still rested.

Too late, Jenny saw she had misjudged the distance between them. To be totally honest, she'd swung her arm toward Joe with some of her frustration behind the gesture, giving it more power and momentum than she'd expected. The pad of her finger mashed against the hardness of solid muscle. She let out a sharp little sound, as if she were the one being jabbed, then froze.

Joe's chin dipped downward. He looked at her pink polished nail pressed to his soft white cotton shirt. Then just as abruptly, he looked up. That smart-guy smile faded instantly from his lips.

His gaze sank into her gaze with a stirring blend of hope and tenderness she'd never seen in him before, or had she simply never let herself see it? Jenny couldn't decide, not with her senses blurred as they were by the long day, the work ahead of her, and the nearness of this man whose chest rose and fell beneath her fingertip.

Jenny wanted to cringe, but she caught herself in time. She would not give him the chance to embarrass her, teasing that it was not miscalculation that had brought her into physical contact with him but her own hidden feelings. She hadn't done it on purpose, after all. The last thing she wanted in this world was for anyone, least of all the man himself, to think there might be any chance of anything ever happening between them.

"Yes, I guess it was lucky I didn't buy the flower," he murmured in a low, distracted tone.

"You got that right, buster." Jenny added a couple more taps with her finger to make it seem like she'd planned that all along, then withdrew. She had not actually intended to touch him, but when she did, she justified that it was only a friendly gesture. It meant nothing. *Then why is my hand trembling?* she wondered as she stepped back and pulled away.

"Um, Jenny?" He leaned in like someone sharing a secret.

"What, Joe?" She edged closer too, unable to help herself.

"*Why* again am I glad I didn't pop for the sunflower boutonniere?"

"Why? Oh…*why!*" That rocketed her back to reality but fast. She tugged at the brim of her hat and stole a fleeting glance over her shoulder at the back door to the wedding chapel, then to the bank clock across the street.

Her pulse surged as if her heart had leapt into her throat.

"I don't have time to play games with you, Joe."

"Gee, and just when I was about to challenge you to hopscotch." He smirked, and as always, the underpinning of sincere humor that always seemed such a part of him took the edge off the sarcasm.

"Funny," Jenny deadpanned. "But the only place I'll be hopping is to the groom's dressing room in the back of the chapel to see if I can salvage—that is, to see if I can do anything to help."

"You said salvage," he accused. "I distinctly heard—"

"Good-bye, Joe. Hope you enjoy the rest of the day's festivities." She waved, more of a swatting motion, really, offered in his general direction, without further eye contact from her. But no sooner had she spun on her heel and started to march off at a frantic pace than she felt Joe at her side, his strides matching hers step for step.

"Mayor Fox, you're keeping something from me, aren't you? What is it? Something to do with the first of the sixty-six hoped-for weddings, I'll bet."

"We don't allow betting in Cupid's Corner, Mr. Avery." She never slowed her pace. Her gaze remained focused on the back corner of the quaint little chapel, though she could not help feeling constantly aware of Joe's closeness. She aimed her feet toward the sidewalk lined with hip-high, prickly shrubbery. "Perhaps you should go back to St. Louis if that's the kind of thing you seek to pursue. I hear they have riverboat gambling on the Mississippi River these days."

"Keeping up with you is gamble enough for me right now, thank you." A green bristled twig slashed against his jeans. He stopped short, then wrangled his way around to the other side of her, catching up in seconds. "So, are you going to tell me what you're up to, just what it is that only our honorable mayor can salvage?"

"I said good-bye." Only a few more yards and she'd be at the door. "Here in this little corner of Kansas the citizenry traditionally considers *good-bye* an end to the conversation, not an invite to tag along."

"And in my circles, which I'll admit consist mainly of newspaper folks and other journalists, a political figure in a rush during a crucial event, tossing out and just as rapidly retracting or evading words like *salvage, problem,* and *fiasco?* That *is* an invite to tag along. No, it's more than an invitation, it's a mandate." He turned the corner with her in tight precision. "I'm sorry, Your Honor, but until I find out exactly what is going on here, I'm sticking to you like glue."

She halted just outside the door and glowered at him. "Glue? If I had guessed, I might have said something a little more disgusting like old gum or something slimy like…like…like some really, really slimy stuff."

Her cheeks flashed hot at her fumbling attempt to put him down. The cool blast of the air conditioning only heightened the sensation as she swung the door open and started inside.

She did not hold the door open for Joe, but he slid through anyway, laughing as he said, "Good command of the language there, Mayor. When your term is over, come and see me about a job on the paper."

"I couldn't possibly accept a job at the *Arrow.*"

"Oh? Why not?" Suspicion colored his words.

"Haven't you heard? The editor there is a bear to work with."

"More like a dog with a bone, especially when he smells a good story. He won't give it up until he's unearthed every last bit of dirt."

"Woof" was all she had to say to that. She had waited long enough for her pupils to adjust to the dim lighting in the back hallway of the old building. Editor sniffing at her heels or not, she had to move now.

Jenny bit her lip and put her hand to her hat, trying to get a better feel for her location. The bride and her attendants, if she had any, had a special dressing room that stretched the length of the left side of the small building. The groom and anyone standing up for him had to get ready in the men's room in the corridor that went to the right of the platform where the ceremonies took place. Jenny just had to remember which hallway led to which room—she dared not alert the bride to this particular problem unless absolutely necessary.

"Let's see, the bride on the left." She gave a wiggle of her left wrist to help her sort through it. "Which from this angle is my right, which means—"

"Which means the problem is with the bride or some member of her party or family?" Joe speculated, even as he took her by the shoulders to point her in the right direction. "Which means we go this way."

"No, I go this way. *You* go that way." She indicated the door they'd come through. "See the pretty red exit sign? It's speaking to you, Joe."

He followed the line of her gesture, twisting his head enough so that she knew he was not watching her.

Seizing the opportunity, she made a dash down the dark hall, feeling only a twinge of guilt that she'd let him assume she wanted to see the bride, then tried to duck away. She had a job to do, just as he did, and she could not let him interfere. Her shoes barely scuffed over the cold linoleum floor as she ran on tiptoe, one hand securing her hat. That she did not hear him pounding down behind her gave her hope that she might scoot inside the groom's dressing room before Joe knew which door she'd taken for sure.

"Men's," she read aloud, half-breathless from the excitement of outsmarting Joe and half-panicked that she'd arrived too late. Without stopping to analyze her actions further, though, she thrust out her hand, palm flat, intent on whisking inside before the newspaper editor tracked her down.

A strong, masculine arm shot past her from behind, the long, blunt fingers circling her wrist before she could even gasp in surprise. "Did I ever mention that I held my high school's record for the hundred-yard dash? Still got what it takes to outrun the best of them, I guess, even if it has been ten years since I won a race."

Jenny wrenched herself free of his amiable grasp. "Did I ever mention to you that I want you to butt out of my business? Why, yes, I believe I did—and it hasn't been any ten years ago! More like ten seconds."

"It's my business to butt into your business, Mayor." He maneuvered himself around her, cutting her off from the door completely. "But that's not the only reason I'm stopping you right now."

"Oh, sure. What other reason would you have for coming between me and my duties other than to get the scoop on a juicy story?"

"How about keeping a friend from making a fool of herself?"

There were so many arguable flaws in that statement that Jenny did not know which to attack first. Prudently, she chose to ignore all of them and press on toward her goal. "Just let me pass. Time is running out, and I have too much on the line."

"I can't, Jenny." She could not see his eyes well in the darkened hallway, so she had to rely on the quiet resonance of his voice to tell her that this was no ploy or joke.

Still, too much was at stake for her to simply give it all

up over the ring of integrity in Joe Avery's words. "Please, Joe. I have to do this."

"Not this way, you don't."

"Stand aside, Joe." She gave him a nudge and he easily moved out of her way. Thankful that common sense had prevailed, she flattened her hand to the door and started to push. "I'm going in."

"Into the *men's* room, Jenny?"

She couldn't have jerked her hand away faster if that door had been on fire. *The men's room!* She hadn't thought about that. No matter how urgent her need to speak to the groom, she could not just barge in there.

"Okay. Obviously, there's some problem regarding the groom. It would hardly take a genius to figure that out by now." He put one hand on her shoulder. "Lucky for me, huh?"

"I wasn't going to say that."

"No. Even when you're furious with me, you'd be far too nice to say that, I know. But you might think it."

She joined him in a soft laugh. "I might think it, but then I might think I didn't have room to criticize, given you just saved me from a less-than-brilliant move myself."

"Glad I could help. It makes me feel good to be able to help you, Jenny."

She caught her breath and held it.

"In fact," he went on, "it makes me feel so good I'd like to offer to do more. If you'd like, I'd be willing to go into no-woman's-land there and ask the groom to come out here to speak to you."

"And you'd stay inside the men's room while he and I talked this through?"

"For a politician, you don't really have a firm handle on you-scratch-my-back, I'll-scratch-yours, do you?"

Her teeth sank into her lower lip, which she envisioned sticking out in a childlike pout. She was certainly acting childish enough, she thought. If nothing else, she owed Joe a debt of gratitude for not having made an issue of that very fact.

She sighed. "I suppose I might as well tell you what's up. If everything works out fine, well, what harm will it do that you got a little inside scoop? It might even make a great hook for the story—and great hooks sell papers and that means more publicity for Cupid's Corner. Besides, if my worst fear comes to pass, you'll know all about it in less than a half-hour anyway."

"Know what?"

"The groom is having second thoughts."

"Is that all?"

"Is that all?" She started to tweak the bulging muscle of his arm, remembered her gut-level reaction to simply touching him by accident, and held back, tugging at his T-shirt sleeve instead. "Is that all? An awful lot is at stake here, pal, and I'm not going to stand by and let some groom with a pair of cold feet ruin it all."

"So you intend to toast his tootsies with your hot temper?"

"His tootsies are safe from me, I promise." She had to smile at his gentle nudge toward a cooler head. "Anyway, I'm not mad, Joe, really. I'm…determined."

"Determined? To do what? Help two people find true happiness or to get the glitch out of your big Hitchin' City celebration?"

"To help the bride and groom, of course!" She shuffled back to put a reasonable distance between them that still enabled them to hear one another speaking in crisp whispers. "Helping this couple comes first. I talked to them last night when they first got into town, Joe. I watched the way they treated each other and listened to their plans for the future. You were there with Larry taking photos for the paper; you saw it."

"Yeah, I have to admit they seemed a really good match, but if the young man is having second thoughts, maybe he shouldn't go through with this."

"The young man is just being immature and selfish. If he'd stop and think this through, he'd do the right thing." She made wide gestures as she spoke, the words coming faster and faster as she tried to make Joe understand the urgency of it all and why she had to intercede now. "If he'd look past his adolescent fear that something better is going to show up around the next corner, or in some other place, then maybe—"

"Whoa there. Hold up a minute." He slashed his hand through the air.

She gulped down a mouthful of cool air and with it the last of her rationalization.

"I understand your point here, Jenny. But don't you think there might be just the slightest possibility that your need to jump in and save this situation comes from your own hidden agenda?"

"A hidden...? Me?" She blinked. "I have no idea what you're talking about."

"C'mon. You and I may joke around with each other about romance and feelings and even that 'man that got away' stuff, Jenny, but you are the last person I know who'd try to kid herself about something so important."

Tension tingled in her scalp and began to slowly work its way down through her body, like a snake coiling tighter and tighter around her.

"Isn't is possible that you feel this extra push to intervene

here and now and get these two married because you could
not do the same thing for yourself two years ago?"

"That is a highly personal assumption to make." And
probably true. She'd never even considered that as a factor
until Joe brought it to her attention. Now, letting the painful
possibility sink slowly into her consciousness, she had to
force herself to admit, it really could be true.

"Am I wrong?" he asked softly.

She shook her head. "No."

"Then maybe someone more impartial should go in and
be the one to remind this reticent groom of all the wonderful reasons for walking down that aisle."

"You?" She had not planned it as an insult, but that's how
the word came out, skeptical and tinged with a hint of a
sneer. Jenny cleared her throat and rushed to clarify. "That is,
what qualifies you to handle a delicate thing like this?"

"I'm a trained listener, Jenny. That's what I do. You've
already pointed out how obviously in love this kid is and
that he's just scared. He doesn't need anyone to talk him back
into this wedding, he needs someone to listen while he talks
himself back into it. *That* I can do."

He had a point. And admitting that, even to herself, did
not lighten Jenny's mood one bit. "But Joe, I—"

"Every minute you stand here and argue is a minute
closer to a bridal march blaring out with no groom waiting
at the altar."

Jenny hesitated.

"Could you just trust me, Jenny? Just this once?"

She shut her eyes. What choice did she have, really?
"I…I guess I'll have to."

"Thatagirl!" He gave her an impromptu hug that lasted
only seconds.

Still, the scent of the sun on his hair, the feel of his arms wound tightly around her lingered with Jenny even as he stepped back toward the closed men's room door and gave her a thumbs-up.

⤟ ⤝

He'd done it. He'd won Jenny's trust—if only on this small thing. Joe squared his shoulders and prepared to make himself a sounding board for a nervous groom. This was his big chance to finally be the hero in Jenny's eyes. He would not let her down.

Ever since Doc Marvelous showed up two weeks ago, Joe had tried everything to win Jenny's attention away from the persistent physician. To her credit, she had not fallen for any of her ex-fiancé's slick lines or smooth tricks—not for the roses he'd had delivered to her office or the way he just seemed to show up at the Wholly Macaroni Pasta Emporium right at twelve-thirty, the exact same time Jenny always stopped in for lunch. Joe had heard about the roses from everyone—no secrets in a town like this—and he'd seen the doctor's cheesy "accidental" meeting ploy at lunch firsthand.

Medical degree or not, the man was not really so smart. Joe had been doing the "just happened to be here, why don't we share a table" technique since the second week he'd been in town, and he'd figured out right away it wasn't going to score him anything more than a pleasant conversation over a plate of pasta. Still, Joe continued to use the trick a couple of times a week, because a good newsman never takes no for an answer, not because he was stubborn or stupid, he always told himself.

Anyway, neither the chance meetings nor the flowers had gotten Michaels anywhere. Jenny kept things curt and

professional, much as she did with Joe. Last month, her attitude had made the newsman crazy, frustrated, and even a
little discouraged. Today, he admired her spunk and even-
tempered handling of things, mostly because it meant that
he and Jenny's ex-fiancé stayed in a dead heat for her affection. But that could all change, starting right now.

All Joe had to do was go in, talk a little sense into this
groom, hear the kid out, and emerge as Jenny's knight in
shining armor, her hero. He squared his shoulders, mentally
trying on the mantle—her hero. He liked it—liked it a lot.
Now all he had to do was earn it.

Joe cleared his throat, cleared his mind as well, then
raised his fist to knock.

Jenny inched forward.

Though he did like the feeling of her standing so close,
he understood that in a town like this it would not do to
have the mayor seen peeking into the men's room, even
under these circumstances. Taking Jenny by the shoulders,
he set her back a few steps. "Give me some room to work my
magic, okay?"

"Okay," she murmured, her lower lip pushed out in just
the hint of a pout.

The position of her mouth made Joe wish he were the
kind of man to press his advantage and steal a kiss. Instead,
he turned away, intent on completing his task. He raised his
arm, aimed his knuckles at the solid wood beneath the men's
room sign, and—

The door swung inward with a whoosh.

If Joe hadn't immediately checked his forward movement, his fisted hand might have landed a blow to the nose
of the man on the other side of the threshold. When Joe saw
who that man was, some little part of him cursed his speedy
reflexes.

"Thank you, Dr. Michaels, thank you for everything," the groom's voice echoed from somewhere in the tiled wash-room.

"Everything is going to be just fine. See you in the chapel in a few minutes." The doctor, dressed in casual clothes that probably cost more than the bridal gown, gave a stiff wave to the unseen groom still inside the room. He turned and scowled at Joe, then at Joe's still-raised fist. Then he looked beyond Joe's shoulder and his face relaxed into a brilliant smile. "Jenny! How nice to find you here!"

Jenny stepped up to the doctor, her fingers toying with the brown hair that fell in waves from beneath her straw hat.

She played with her hair when she worried what people thought of her, Joe had noticed. She used to do it around him all the time. He clenched his jaw.

"How...amazing to find you here, Alex."

"Amazing? Not at all."

Annoying would be a better word for it, Joe thought, but withheld his opinion.

"Someone from the chapel called me over. It seems the groom had an anxiety attack." Alex gave what could only be described as a benevolent smile.

It grated on Joe's nerves. He gritted his teeth into a smile of his own and said, "So we heard. In fact, I was just going to go in and see what I could do to calm him down and get him headed down the aisle."

Michaels shifted his weight, entirely blocking Joe's access to the door. "Don't bother, I've already taken care of every-thing."

"You have?" There was a softly adoring tone in Jenny's voice that did nothing to soothe Joe's irritation with this sit-uation.

"Sure. It was no big deal, really, just handed the young

man a paper bag to breathe into so he wouldn't hyperventilate."

"Ahh, the wonders of modern medicine," Joe grumbled.

"Less modern medicine and more old-fashioned common sense." Alex answered Joe's sarcasm, but he spoke only to Jenny. "The fellow just needed someone to listen while he sorted through his problems and misgivings."

It was a hollow victory to Joe that his solution had worked. After all, it had worked to make the wrong man the hero in Jenny's eyes. Joe made a fast study of the woman with the face straight out of a dream and a strong personality out of some men's nightmares.

Jenny's overall character was no nightmare to him. He loved the way she stood up for her town and stood up to anyone who threatened it. He valued her unreasonable sense of responsibility mixed with her sentimental notions about home and family and preserving what's good and right for generations to come. He liked watching her march up the steps of City Hall to work on Monday and watching her sing in the church choir on Sunday. He respected that she did not fall in love easily, nor let go of love lightly.

He hated that he saw that very fact reflected in her eyes right now as she looked up at Dr. Alex Michaels.

"So, you listened to the groom while he talked himself back into getting married?" Jenny whispered.

"Yes. Yes, I did." Alex beamed with self-sure pride.

How could he not see, Joe wondered, the flash of pain in Jenny's wonderful eyes? How could he, of all people, not know how much that proclamation from him would reopen the old heartaches and questions for her?

He wanted to put his hand on Jenny's back, to give her some sign of his emotional support, but he knew it would not be welcomed. So he laughed and tried to make a joke instead. "I thought you had the guy breathing into a paper bag. Doesn't seem like he'd get in much gab time that way."

"Well, you've got me there, Avery." He said Joe's name hard, much the way Joe said *Michaels* whenever he spoke directly to the man he thought of as his romantic rival. "I guess I did do a little talking of my own. I suppose I felt I had some special insight into his particular frame of mind."

"Alex," Jenny said softly. She bowed her head. "I'm not sure I want to hear this."

Joe stepped forward. This time he did put one hand on her back and gripped her shoulder with the other. "You don't have to do anything you don't want to do, Jenny. The wedding is going to start in a few minutes. Maybe we should go take our seats."

She wet her lips, her eyes still downcast, then exhaled and lifted her chin. "Yes. Thank you, Joe. Maybe we should…"

Her words trailed off as she let Joe turn her to the hallway that led toward the small chapel, probably filled to capacity. They had only taken a step or two when Michaels's words came after them.

"I told the groom I knew what he was contemplating. That I'd walked a mile in his rented dress shoes, as it were."

Jenny stopped.

"We don't want to be late," Joe urged.

She nodded and started to walk again.

Again, her ex-fiancé's voice followed them. "I told him I'd chosen to pursue my own immature, self-indulgent way—and that those selfish wishes cost my bride-to-be a lot of grief and embarrassment."

Jenny's footsteps faltered.

"What do you want to do, Jenny?" It was not an easy thing for Joe to ask, but he had to. He had to let her act on whatever was best for her, not for what his own ego or feelings desired.

Jenny inched her chin up farther and sighed. She shut her eyes. No tears lined her thick lashes. No tremor made the grim line of her mouth quiver. She seemed truly more tired than touched, more disconcerted than depressed.

Had Joe read her all wrong? She'd claimed she no longer had feelings for the man who'd once held her heart but had cruelly discarded it for his own admittedly selfish reasons.

"Let's go to the wedding, Joe." Jenny took his arm without looking back. "Everyone will be waiting."

Joe stood a little taller. He stuck his chest out a little more. Maybe things hadn't turned out too bad, after all. Maybe this incident had rung the death knell for Jenny's old feelings for Dr. Michaels.

"One more thing I told him, Jenny," Michaels called out. "I think you should know. After I told him all that I just told you, I had one more thing to say—that walking away from my own wedding had been the biggest mistake of my life."

Jenny's fingernails sank into Joe's bare arm, and though she continued to walk stiffly on down the hall at Joe's side, he knew. No way was this thing between Jenny and Alex over.

Well, that might be, Joe thought, but no way was he giving up either. If Jenny wanted Alex, she'd be with Alex right now. But it was Joe's arm she was on tonight, and he was going to do everything he could from now on to make sure she stayed there.

To the People of Cupid's Corner,
Hitchin' City, USA
The Wedding Capital of Route 66
and to all the couples who began their
happily-ever-afters in this place:

We celebrate the bond unbroken,
Given with the vows you've spoken,
And pray that all who here pledge their love,
will find God's blessing from above.
And for those hearts still lost and lonely,
that here you'll find your one and only.

—engraved on the brass plaque at the base of the statue of
Cupid on the lawn of City Hall in the town square

Five

I told him it was the biggest mistake I'd ever made." Alex's confession still rang in Jenny's ears. She climbed onto the back of the flatbed truck that had served as a makeshift grandstand during the Fourth of July parade this morning, then later provided a stage for a performance by the Mighty Archers High School Jazz Band during the wedding reception. Now, with night closing in, it would provide an excellent vantage point from which to view the fireworks.

By tradition and for safety reasons—they didn't want to have a child or older person hurt at the festivities—only single adults were allowed the benefit of spreading their blankets on the truck bed to watch the show. It was no small joke around town that they parked the truck this close to the nine-foot-tall bronze Cupid that graced the center of the lawn to encourage those singles to become couples.

As mayor, Jenny's place was here, though she'd much rather have been anywhere else. Home came to mind, curled up in her real bed with the covers pulled over her head. And she'd like to stay that way until all her feelings of indecisiveness and confusion had completely ebbed—sometime around Groundhog Day at the earliest.

The smell of hay bales, stacked up as a staircase and scattered around the courthouse lawn as seating, tingled in her nose. She adjusted her hat, giving her scalp a welcome scratch. The commotion of the gathering crowd, spilling out from the wedding chapel after the reception she and the town council had sponsored, did not blot out the hard thudding of her pulse in her ears.

She scanned the grounds, which blurred to a confetti of red, white, and blue in her mind, looking for—

She spotted Alex shaking the groom's hand. Her heart stopped, and she suspected only one kind of doctor could do anything to help her get it going again. She sighed. How handsome Alex looked, how tall and dashing, like a man who had just stepped from the pages of a catalogue or even a romance novel. Gorgeous. Intelligent. Perfect.

"And entirely out of place in this little hick town," she muttered under her breath to no one in particular, though she did rather imagine herself confiding in the Cupid leering down over her shoulder. "Nothing has changed since he chose the city and the life it had to offer over me and Cupid's Corner. I still have too many obligations here, and this town is still about as interesting as mud to a guy like Alex. Nothing has changed…unless Alex himself has changed."

She studied the ease with which he now moved, the way he sought out old friends among the crowd. Even Nurse Pritchet seemed to have warmed to him, or at least reached an understanding that he would not let her run his life as she did Doc's. Maybe Jenny was the one making the mistake now, she thought, folding her arms and cocking her head, as if the new angle might help her to better see beneath Alex's facade. Maybe she should spend more time with Alex, indulge her curiosity and his perseverance, and allow herself to get reacquainted with the man. Maybe if she gave him another chance she'd find out—

"He's full of surprises, isn't he?"

Jenny jumped. Her hand grabbed her hat to keep it from falling off. For a fraction of a second, she thought her bronze companion had answered her back, and just as quickly the reality of who had spoken took hold.

"Joe! You scared the living daylights out of me!" Jenny clutched at her hat brim and spun around on her heel to face the newspaper editor, who must have crept onto the flatbed platform for no better purpose than to startle her half out of her skin. "Don't you ever sneak up on me like that again."

"I didn't sneak anywhere, I just—" He whipped his head around to peer at the spot where Jenny had been staring moments earlier. "Ah, I see. You were so distracted by young Doctor Killjoy over there that you didn't even hear me walk up behind you."

"I…" She wouldn't lie, but she hardly wanted to stand there and divulge her innermost thoughts. Not to Joe—not about Alex. So she decided to change the subject instead. "*Who's* full of surprises?"

Joe eyed her for one long, silent moment, then sighed, shrugged, and jerked his thumb over his shoulder toward the statue. "Ol' Bow Boy there."

Jenny slowly turned to face the icon which she'd pretty much taken for granted her entire life. "You mean Cupid?"

"That's the one." Joe nodded and crossed his arms. The pale blue bride's garter, which he'd caught at the wedding, expanded around his flexed biceps, accenting the muscle. "Did you know that this work of, um, for lack of a better word, *art*—"

He stopped to grin at her, the way a man smiles over

some goofy trophy or object of pride and affection that is admittedly silly or showy.

Any animosity or snobbery Jenny might have attached to the jest about the unusual landmark vanished with Joe's guileless expression. She had no doubt he sincerely loved the diaperclad likeness of the town's namesake just as much as any native.

"Did you know the bronze beauty here was donated by an elderly widow?" he asked with a tip of his head.

"Uh, yes, that does sound familiar. She and her husband had eloped here, I believe."

Joe nodded. "Eloped because after waiting years for the man everyone told her she should marry to finally make the big commitment, she woke up one day and realized she loved the boy next door."

"She did?" Jenny strained her brain to recall this bit of local history. Surely she would have heard it somewhere before. Unless, of course, Joe was making it all up to try to persuade her, yet again, to go out with him. She started to tell him she was on to his trick, but he rushed on before she could say another word.

"Yes, she did. She'd always loved him and he had always loved her, and they'd both grown old while she chased after someone who would never make her happy." He raised his eyebrows; no mischief glimmered in the depths of his eyes.

Jenny glanced around them. The sky had grown darker. The crowd had grown large and boisterous. Though a few people had taken up spots on the truck around where they stood, she felt as if no one else in town existed, as if she and Joe were alone and everything beyond them was just noise and hazy color.

"They eloped because she didn't want to waste another minute of their life together waiting on anything, not even a fancy wedding." Joe shifted, and his athletic shoes crunched over a few yellow straws of hay beneath his feet. "They were married for only a few years when he died unexpectedly."

"How awful."

"The widow said she felt truly grateful for whatever time they had been given together. So, she proposed and donated this monument to Cupid's Corner."

"Because the place held special memories? Because it was where they finally got married?"

"That's part of it, of course. But she also liked the idea of it being in a place with such a romantic name, where the marriage commitment is celebrated in the name of every business downtown, that kind of thing."

"Guess she didn't think those names were all that corny," Jenny teased.

"Hey, to be fair, this thing was built thirty years ago, long before anyone came up with names like Wholly Macaroni Pasta Emporium or Tie the Knot Menswear. She didn't have the burden of having to use those labels in legitimate news pieces every week." He frowned, trying to look quite serious.

Jenny laughed.

He rolled his eyes to show his disgust, then lowered his short black lashes so he looked to be stealing a sly sideways glance.

Jenny's breath snagged in her throat. She patted the silky hair hanging down snug against her neck, held in place by the tilt of her hat.

"But there's another reason she wanted to put this statue here, Jenny. Probably the most important reason of all." Joe stroked the curve of the readied bronze bow. "The woman who funded this piece said she wanted it to encourage people to be more aware of all the opportunities for love around them every day."

He stood so close that despite the fading light, she could see the blush of sun on the bridge of his nose and the shadow of the day's-end beard on his chin and jawline. She could feel the slow, measured rhythm of his breathing. She noticed that even though he was not yet thirty, a few strands of silver laced through his thick black hair.

In some strange way that only enhanced his story. It underscored the fact that time was flying. They were neither one as young as they had been and so many…opportunities, as Joe had called them, had already passed.

"I…I never knew…" she whispered, then, hearing the breathless quality of her speech, coughed lightly and added, "about the statue. I never knew any of that about it at all."

"If you knew, it wouldn't be surprising, now would it?" He touched his fingertip to her nose, then dropped his hand to his side. "Furthermore, this widow wrote the poem on the plaque herself."

"Now, *that's* not so surprising." She spoke up to be heard over the crackling static of the nearby speaker, which would soon blast out patriotic music to embellish the fireworks show. "I didn't think it was Shakespeare."

He conceded her point with a wink that hinted at a shared secret.

Her heart skipped a beat. She blamed the sudden *tweep* screeching from the antiquated sound system, but deep down, she knew better.

"Well, you can't fault the dear for trying," he said. "Besides, she wanted some very specific references for the monument. She included the mention of God, for example, to show that love and commitment come from—and grow with—the Lord and are not just some quirk of fate or the result of Cupid's arrow."

"What? No trace of cynicism at that kind of thinking?"

His openness and candor intrigued Jenny. She whisked off her hat and tossed back her hair.

He stretched out his hand with such perfect timing that the last shake of her head brought her cheek to rest gently in his warm palm. His eyes searched hers. "Why should there be?"

She opened her mouth, sighed, then shrugged. "You don't usually associate big-city reporter types with championing the forever-after route. You know, what God has joined together let no man put asunder, that type of thing. It doesn't suit the stereotype."

"First, I was raised in a household with a strong sense of family and faith. I hope to have the same in my own home someday—with the right woman." He left his hand on her face and held her eyes with his gaze.

The only thing weaker than Jenny's knees just then were her vocal cords. She simply stood there, looking at this Joe, wondering if she knew him at all, and listened and learned.

"And second…" He pulled his hand away, and his eyes took on that old accustomed flash of fun. "In case you haven't noticed, this is not a big city, Your Honor, and I am an editor, not a reporter. So even if that stereotype held true, it would not apply to me, not anymore. Cupid's Corner is my home now, and I plan to stay here and in this job for a very long time."

"You do?" She fingered the brim of the hat she held in front of her.

"What? No cynicism for *that*?"

She laughed to hear her words thrown back at her so appropriately. "Actually, I was just thinking that—what did you call him—Bow Boy? I was thinking he isn't the only one full of surprises."

He accepted her observation with a quick duck of his head.

She smiled.

He smiled back, only not so broadly.

She fumbled with her hat, not sure what more to do or say.

"Speaking of Bow Boy, here," he said, casually filling the awkward silence between them. "Did you also know that since the woman who commissioned him married too late in life to have children, she asked the sculptor to use both her features and her husband's to suggest what a child of theirs might have looked like?"

Jenny lifted her chin to peer up at the cherubic face.

"And furthermore, she stipulated that the pose must include the bow drawn and arrow always at the ready. She wanted that to stand as a reminder to everyone who passes by that love may find you any minute now."

Jenny's gaze dipped to the arrow, which, because they stood on the truck bed, was now level with her hip. But from the usual vantage on the courthouse lawn, the thing did point downward at such an angle that one could easily imagine it hitting an unsuspecting passerby right in the heart. She shook her head. "I never knew all this."

"Read this week's paper. It'll all be in there and then some." The loudspeaker crackled again, and he leaned forward and raised his voice to make himself heard above it. "I'm rerunning the original article from the dedication ceremony."

"You are?" Jenny spoke up too. "Why?"

"I thought you'd be pleased." He tucked his hands in his jeans pockets, his shoulders hunched defensively.

"Oh, I am. I am!" she rushed to reassure him. "It's just that, it's so helpful to the whole wedding project and falls right in with my vision of promoting the town. I certainly never expected that kind of cooperation from you, after you'd made your opinion of my plans so—"

"Hey, your ideas might not be what I'd pick, Jenny, but they are what the town has chosen to go with. I want to support this place. It's my home now, and I'd never sabotage anything that might help people here."

"I know that, Joe." And she did. She knew it down to the center of her being. She also knew she had no business gazing dreamily into Joe Avery's amazing dark eyes. Least of all, standing in the dead center of town, on a raised platform with a great big Cupid as a backdrop. "Joe, I...I think I'd better go—"

"But the fireworks haven't even begun."

He obviously had no idea what was going on inside her heart, she thought. Nothing less than a full-scale volley of explosives could create the wildly erratic interplay of emotions she now felt—bright and thrilling one moment, smoky and terrifying the next.

Joe reached for her hand. "You have to stay for the fireworks show. It's the grand finale to the whole day."

She deftly slipped her hand away before he could get a firm grasp. Her fingertips tingled from the new sensation of brushing over his work-roughened palm. Her mind raced to try to come up with an excuse that would neither encourage nor offend him. "I can watch the show from some other spot. That is, I thought I might find my sister and nephew. Her husband had to go to bed early tonight because he's going out of town for work tomorrow, and so Bobbie Ann has the baby here alone and—"

"But what about the town tradition? Aren't you, as mayor, honor-bound to watch the fireworks right here with all the other eligible singles?" He swept his hand out, and for the first time Jenny realized that several other people had joined them on the flatbed. "If you don't have a blanket to sit on, good ol' Pritchy sent me off with a great big comfy quilt.

89

I think I could be persuaded to share. If you promise to behave yourself, that is."

She crushed the straw brim in her hands until woven fibers crinkled. "I don't think so."

"All right then. *Don't* behave yourself. That'll make for a way better story in the next paper anyway." He stretched out his hands as if reading a headline unfurled before them. "Mayor Runs Amuck at Annual Festivities: Sits on Same Quilt as Former City Slicker!"

"So, you *do* see the kind of scandal it could create." She played along.

"No more so than 'Fearful Mayor Flees Fourth Festivities.'" He made short, precise gestures as if placing each stinging word of that make-believe heading in front of her.

"Say that three times fast," she challenged, in hopes he'd get the message and drop it.

"Stay, Jenny. It's just a fireworks show."

Easy for him to say, she thought; the only fireworks he had to contend with were in the sky.

"It's not like you don't have the whole town acting as chaperone, you know."

"Oh, now you're really sweetening the pot. A flatbed truck and crazy quilt and thee—*the* entire population of my constituents, that is." She laughed, but as she glanced around them, she became more aware than ever of how many people clustered here and there waiting for the show that would start at any minute. More than one pair of eyes already had targeted her and Joe, no doubt speculating whether they'd see some kind of show there as well.

"What can happen?" Joe asked. He gave the statue directly behind her a pat. "Unless, of course, you're afraid that our bronze buddy might stir up a little romance between us."

"Ha!" She said it with far more bravado than she felt.

"Well, it is a beautiful starlit night, we are two young, single, and relatively attractive people—"

"How you do flatter a girl," she muttered.

Unfazed, Joe went on, "And he *is* Cupid, after all."

She flung out the hand clutching her hat. "*He* is a chunk of molded metal alloy."

"Don't listen to her," Joe spoke directly to the statue. "She's just worried. The romantic in her, deep, deep down in her—way beyond the self-sacrificing mayor mode—that part of her is worried that one shot from your arrow there will send her helplessly into the arms of Mr. Right."

Jenny craned her neck enough to peer over her shoulder and toss off a remark to the statue too. "The only thing that worries me is that the town newspaper editor has taken up talking to lawn ornaments. As for your arrow having any effect on me—fat chance, Bow Boy! I am not interested in any romantic entanglements right now."

"Not *any?*" Joe's sober expression directed her attention to his line of vision.

Alex bent at the waist, more of a rigid bow, really, and tousled the mop of red hair on a passing child. While the gesture looked awkward, the effect came off smooth as silk. He flashed that dazzling doctor smile of his, the way a policeman uses a badge to get onlookers to back down, thus deftly sidestepping a conversation with the boy's mother as he did. Clearly, Alex aimed to keep his level of involvement with the people of Cupid's Corner professional and very shallow.

Sensing this only added to Jenny's confusion. In the chapel hallway he'd sounded sincerely filled with regret, so...changed. But as she stood back to observe him, if anything, he seemed more removed than ever from the things she loved.

What did it all mean? she wondered. How was she supposed to deal with all the emotional turmoil he—and if she
was honest, Joe, too—created in her? That and help save the
town she loved with this summer's promotional events? She
couldn't.

"Let me assure you, Joe, that the last thing on earth I
want is to get involved with any man this summer. Now if
you'll excuse me—"

"Jenny, wait!" Joe lurched toward her.

"Jenny! Jenny! There you are. I've been looking all over
for you!" Alex shouted to make himself heard from the
ground as he rushed to the truck.

A booming march blared from the loudspeaker, and the
man staging the evening fireworks show barked out a blus-
tery welcome. "In just a few moments we will be turning out
the streetlights all around the town square so everyone can
get a real good view of the show. So get yourselves situated
now, folks."

Joe reached for her elbow. "Jenny, I think you should—"

"Wait right there, Jenny, I'll join you," Alex demanded.

Despite the perfect temperatures and the pleasant
evening breeze, Jenny felt hot. She couldn't breathe. All she
wanted was to get away so she could think, so she could col-
lect herself and put aside all this talk of romance, regrets, and
Mr. Right.

Alex climbed aboard the flatbed at the end farthest from
where she and Joe now stood.

Joe cupped her elbow in his hand and tugged.

She couldn't take this. She had to be alone now; that was
all she knew. She jerked her arm away from Joe's touch.
"Look, all I want to do right now is get off this truck. Would
you just stop pawing at me and let me go?"

"Pawing at you?" Joe looked genuinely hurt at that. "I

was hardly pawing at you, Jenny. I was trying to keep you from—"

"Is he bothering you, Jenny?" Alex called as he tried to pick his way through the patchwork of blankets to reach her.

"And now let's get tonight's festivities off to a start with a real bang!" the announcer bellowed.

The streetlights framing the town square went off, plunging them all into pitch darkness.

This was her chance to slip away unnoticed, Jenny decided. But she had to act fast: Any second now the sky would light with fireworks and she'd be seen. She extended her foot to help gauge the edge of the truck, then took a cautious step backward, away from Joe.

The high-pitched whistle of a rocket soaring skyward pierced the air.

"Eeoow!" Jenny let out a shriek of her own, her hand immediately seeking the place where an icy point had jabbed her backside.

"Jenny!" the two men cried out simultaneously.

Jenny leapt forward in the darkness, realizing too late that she could fall off the truck and be seriously injured. She held her breath.

A pair of strong masculine arms caught her and kept her on her feet, enfolding her in soothing safety.

Overhead…a sputter…a bang…then a great burst illuminated everything below in a glimmering shower of glorious white light. And there she stood, at the center of town on a platform, sent into the arms of Joe Avery by none other than Cupid's arrow!

God Bless This Mess!

—*sign hanging on Jenny Fox's front door*

Six

"Thank you for walking home with me from downtown, Bobbie Ann." Jenny slid the key into the lock, churned it hard to one side, gave it a jiggle. The worn latch released and the forty-year-old door drooped open.

"No problem, sweetie. Since the noise upset the baby so much, I was glad to get away early." Bobbie Ann kissed the temple of the eighteen-month-old little boy, Danny, balanced on her hip.

He snuggled sleepily against her neck and popped his thumb into his mouth.

The sight warmed Jenny's heart and put her petty problems in perspective. Compared to raising a family, providing them with food and shelter, and nurturing a child emotionally and spiritually, having too many men interested in her was not exactly cause for distress. It wasn't life and death or even sickness and health. Compared to the job she'd taken on as mayor, to help the people she cared about make decent lives for themselves and their families and give them the promise of a good future, her chaotic love life was small potatoes.

She slid her hand along the wall to flip on the living-room light before nudging the door open and stepping inside. It still gave her such comfort to walk into the house she had grown up in and call it home. She would always feel grateful for the childhood she'd shared here with her sister and for the loving parents she'd known. She'd made a good decision in buying the place and staying here, where she belonged.

Unlike Alex, she had no regrets about the past—unless it was the immediate past—say, the last half-hour or so. She rubbed her hand over what she suspected would turn into a purple-and-blue bruise high on her hip and sighed. She still couldn't believe she'd just dashed off the platform without another word to either Joe or Alex, leaving both men calling after her. Her cheeks grew hot just imagining what people were probably already saying about the whole peculiar incident.

She raised her hand to her head to whisk away her hat, then realized she'd left that behind too, along with pretty much most of her dignity. She exhaled a long, huffing breath that did nothing to alleviate the tightness in her chest. What a perfect fool she'd made of herself tonight!

Bobbie Ann crossed the threshold, still talking and cooing to young Danny. They made such a lovely picture, so sweet, so happy. Jenny's heart swelled at the sight and at the thought that this was why she had to press on, despite her personal discomfort.

As mayor, she had a job to do, after all, and people looking to her leadership for hope and solutions. If she was smart, she'd put all this concern over the nonsense with Joe and Alex out of her mind and focus on what really mattered.

Jenny's teeth sank into her lower lip even as her mouth curved into a big smile. "Okay, who wants ice cream?"

"We really can't." Bobbie Ann shook her head. "The baby is so tired."

"Just one scoop? On a cone?"

"It's tempting, but we have to get up bright and early tomorrow morning to see Daddy off on another business trip, don't we, sugarpie?" She stroked her knuckle over Danny's pink cheek.

"I'll bet you get tired of Mark going off so much for his work." Jenny leaned back against the ugly old brown-and-white-checked wallpaper she should have stripped off the first few weeks after her parents had moved away.

"Actually, it's been the primary topic of discussion around our house the last few weeks. You know, trying to find the best way to cope, thinking of what's best for Danny—"

"Sure you have to do that." Jenny scuffed the toe of her tennis shoe on the rust-flecked brown carpet, a remnant of the autumn-toned motif her mom had preferred. "But in the end it can't be helped, I guess, Mark's traveling and all. What can you do? His work takes him away, and your heart keeps you here. I sure know how that goes."

"Mark and I are not exactly the same as you and Alex, you know, Jenny."

"Oh, I know. You're happy!" She stroked her nephew's plump little leg. "And you're still together."

"Ye-es." Bobbie Ann drew the word out a bit too long for Jenny's comfort.

Her throat constricted and her hand went to her sister's shoulder. "You are happy, aren't you? You'd tell me if there were anything wrong, wouldn't you?"

"Of course, Jenny. We're very happy."

"Oh. Oh, good. It's just that I sensed some…reticence, I suppose." And to Jenny's way of thinking that included her sister's expression and actions as much as the inflection and hesitation in her voice.

Bobbie Ann lingered in the doorway, hugging her child

close and swaying gently to keep him drowsy and content. Clearly, she did not want to come in and sit awhile and visit. If she did, she felt comfortable enough in this house to barge right on in, plop down, and put her feet up anywhere she desired. No, her sister was holding back, and that made Jenny nervous.

"I...I guess maybe if you sensed something in me it was..." She would not look Jenny in the eye. In fact she seemed overly fascinated by the downy blond hair on her son's head.

"Go on, Bobbie Ann, you can tell me anything."

"I know I can tell you anything. This is just...well, it's just some news I'm not sure I'm ready to share."

"No! Oh, Bobbie Ann, you're going to have another baby!" Jenny started to wrap her sister in a big hug, but Bobbie Ann stuck out a hand to stop her.

"If we are, it's news to me!" She laughed. "Actually, I don't see how we'll ever be able to have another baby as long as Mark travels so much. Not with all the difficulties I had in my first pregnancy. Beyond that, I could never take care of two children—not being alone so much."

"Don't say that, hon. You'd have me around and all your friends. Living in a place like this, you're never really alone. Everyone is always close by to keep an eye on things." Her thoughts flashed back to the calamity on the flatbed with everyone looking on. She'd hear about that tomorrow, she could count on it. And the day after and the day after that—probably years from now it would still be a favorite Fourth of July story in the tiny town. "No, in a town this size, you're never really alone—even when you wish you could be."

"Having friends and even a sister around is not the same as having a husband—and a daddy—around, Jenny. You have to appreciate that."

"Yes, I suppose, but—"

"That's played a big part in our decision."

It saddened Jenny to think her sister could let circumstances rule such a meaningful part of her life. Bobbie Ann and Mark had always wanted a big family. Now she seemed to be saying that Mark's work and her desire to stay here were denying them that dream. "Oh, Bobbie Ann, I hate to think that you won't have any more children—"

"Who said anything about not having any more children?" The sharpness and volume of her tone startled the baby. His big eyes flew open. Bobbie Ann caressed his head softly to lull him back to his half-sleep and whispered, "I never said we wouldn't have more children. But the truth is, we won't have any as long as we keep our home here in Cupid's Corner."

"What are you saying?" Jenny instinctively knew what her sister was struggling to tell her, but she had to hear it outright, to make sure she had not misread the message again.

"Jenny, Mark has a job offer in a suburb of Kansas City. That's where he's going tomorrow, to take one last tour and go over the signing package."

"He…he's going to take the job?"

"He wouldn't have to travel anymore. It would mean he'd be home for dinner every night and there to tuck the baby in and—"

"He is going to take the job." Jenny's mind spun. First Alex had left to live elsewhere, then her parents had moved away for her father's health, and now Bobbie Ann? It just seemed too much. The reality weighed on her like a heavy stone on her chest. "B-but this is your home."

"And it still will be. It always will be." Bobbie Ann placed her hand on Jenny's arm and gave a light squeeze. "We'll come back to visit often, I promise."

"That's not the same as living here, Bobbie Ann," she barely managed to whisper. "I feel like you're going off like everyone else and leaving me behind to—"

"You chose to stay behind, Jenny." Big-sister concern colored her swift but gentle correction of the way Jenny saw things. "It's always been your choice, hon. You could have married Alex and gone with him two years ago, but you chose not to leave."

"I stayed because you needed me, Bobbie Ann," Jenny said. "Granted, that wasn't the only reason, but—"

"You stayed because you wanted to, Jenny." Her sister's back straightened like a cat's back pricked up to anticipate a fight. She spoke softly, though, and let the truth of what she had to say carry the force of her conviction. "Don't blame anyone but yourself for that. You could go anywhere you want, anytime you want. Look at you, you became a mayor before your twenty-seventh birthday—you could do anything you really wanted to."

It comforted Jenny somewhat to hear the pride shining through her sister's reproach.

"What you wanted to do was stay here, Jenny. That's the only reason you're still here, because it's where you want to be more than anything. You love this town and everything about it, and you want to stay here and fight to keep it, and its lifestyle, alive and thriving."

Much as she appreciated her sister's thoughts on this matter, Jenny had other realities to consider. "Thank you for what sounds like a vote of confidence, sweetie, but what I want, my hopes and dreams, simply aren't going to be enough in this case. To be blunt, how can Cupid's Corner survive if people like you and Mark and even Alex keep leaving, Bobbie Ann?"

"I don't know—maybe you could make a bigger contribution to the effort." Her sister's eyes sparked with a hint of teasing.

"Me? What more could I do? I've already dedicated all my working hours and most of my free time to the cause, to the big summer plans, to PR efforts—" She ran her hand back through her hair, her bare head reminding her of one more thing she'd given up to the cause. "Not to mention that I lost my favorite hat tonight in what pretty much amounted to a big clown act for the whole town."

"I wasn't talking about hats or publicity or even the mayorship, Jenny."

"Then what?" She scrunched up her brow, trying to imagine what her sister meant. "What more could I do to help the town thrive and grow the population?"

"Oh, I don't know," she said like someone who knew exactly what she'd recommend. Bobbie Ann laid her cheek on her son's head. "But they say any good leader should have his—or her—own house in order first, before trying to tell others how to tend to theirs. Maybe you should start this 'rebuilding of the town' by marrying and having children of your own? That's one thing you could do to increase the population."

"Marry and have—" She rolled her eyes. "Not like I haven't tried to take that route once already—with less than sterling results, I might add. Besides, marriage and children are not something I can simply go out and do all on my own, even if I wanted to."

"Then maybe you should start by trying to be a little nicer to the new people who move here—and the ones who move back."

"You mean Joe and Alex?"

"Joe and Alex." Bobbie Ann nodded.

"I'm not sure what you're driving at." Jenny gathered her dark curls in one hand at the back of her neck, then smoothed her palm down over her hair and let it fall loose again. "But if you're suggesting that I chase after either one of those…those…"

"Wonderful men?" Bobbie Ann hastened to supply.

"I don't think I'd call either of them wonderful," Jenny snapped.

"Then how about upstanding, educated, caring, hard-working, not-too-hard-on-the-ol'-eyeballs examples of man-liness?" Bobbie Ann grinned. "You could do worse than to give one of them a chance, Jenny."

"I wouldn't even…I couldn't! I mean Joe is…Let's not even talk about it. And Alex? He chose a location over mar-riage to me."

"Just like you did to him."

"I did no such thing!"

"Didn't you?"

Jenny opened her mouth to insist she had not, but she just could not do it. For the first time she looked at what had happened from that perspective, with eyes not clouded by hurt, disappointment, or indignation. "You know, you're right. I did the same thing to Alex that I've held against him all this time."

"Well, not the *exact* same thing."

"Why didn't I see this before? Why didn't you point it out to me?"

"Well, maybe because it isn't really the same thing, Jenny. Alex had promised you he'd live in Cupid's Corner when you two made your marriage plans. He let you go ahead with that assumption, knowing he'd already applied for a position in Kansas City, knowing he would accept the job if it was offered. You were up-front with him, but he wasn't with you."

The explanation rushed out as if Bobbie Ann were trying to quickly gloss over the new concept of Alex forming in Jenny's mind. "Jenny, honey, he hurt you, and I for one can't stand here and say I don't think he'd do it again."

"I probably hurt Alex just as much as he did me, you know." Jenny bowed her head. "My refusal to go with him had to feel like a kind of rejection. It had to have caused him some grief, even if he did still elect to move on."

"Yes, he moved on, not just from your relationship, but he moved away—because that's what *he* wanted. Don't kid yourself, Jenny, don't convince yourself of something just because you hope for it so much or because it might take some of the sting out of a hurt you've harbored for two years." Her sister drew herself up as much as she could with a child sleeping on her shoulder. "I certainly have no reason to think that Alex is back in our...in this 'one-horse town without the horse' for good."

"I have no reason to think he's here for anything but good, Bobbie Ann." *I told him it was the biggest mistake I'd ever made.* Alex's claim echoed through her mind. Her thoughts swam with the possibilities that this discussion had just opened up to her. "Alex came back to town to pitch in when it had no personal benefit for him. He would only do that if he truly cared about this place."

"Or someone in it."

Jenny couldn't help but smile. She did not think she still had feelings for Alex, especially not romantic feelings, not a rekindling of true love. Yet as she stood here thinking about it, she had butterflies in her stomach. "You sound as confused about Alex's motives and our potential together as I feel, sis."

"No, Jenny, when I said Alex might have taken on the job here for someone he cared about, I meant Doc."

The butterflies turned to stone, a cold, grim weight in her midsection. "But a minute ago you told me I should be nicer to Alex—"

"And Joe," Bobbie Ann added.

"You lumped it in with a bunch of talk about marriage and children and growing the town by keeping certain people happy, specifically Alex—"

"And *Joe*."

"Bobbie Ann! No! You can*not* be encouraging me to…you can't possibly be hinting that I should go out with Joe Avery? With Joe?"

"No, I'm not hinting. I'm saying it outright. Go out with Joe Avery, Jenny." She enunciated each syllable of the last sentence as if it had to be unmistakably sounded out for her dense sister. "Go out with Alex, too, if you feel so inclined. But please keep in mind that Alex broke your heart."

"Like I could ever forget that," Jenny muttered. "The man didn't just leave me behind, he fibbed to me, and when I refused to go along with his change of plans, he left me standing there sniffling into my toilet-paper wedding dress. Nothing will ever erase that from my mind, believe me."

"Well, as long as you're smart about it, maybe you could give him another chance."

"Wait a minute, I thought you were on the pro-Joe ticket."

Bobbie Ann laughed. "I'm on the what's-best-for-Jenny ticket. And what's best for you is to open yourself up to romance. Don't cut yourself off from love entirely. Before you know it, it may be too late."

Shades of the story Joe had shared with her, about the woman who dedicated the Cupid statue, came back to haunt

Jenny. She chewed at her lower lip. "But Joe, Bobbie Ann? Joe? He's so—"

"Cute?"

He was that, in his own rumpled, sort of brash-young-buck way. Jenny pictured him sitting in on the town council meeting, all smart remarks and smirking looks. She shook her head. "He's arrogant."

"He's confident," Bobbie Ann amended.

"He's a wise guy."

"Yes, the man has made some pretty smart moves since he got here, I'll give him that." Bobbie Ann kissed her sleeping son's forehead, which did not conceal the grin twitching on her lips. "And he's made quite a few friends, too. He's a regular charmer."

Jenny thought of how Joe had won over stern Nurse Pritchet, and how he made the people on the council laugh, but sometimes at the expense of her projects and suggestions. "He's not a charmer, he needs a charmer—a snake charmer or somebody who can take him to task and keep his manners and ego in check."

"I agree. I also think that *somebody* could be—"

Jenny's hand shot up, and she turned her head away in a bit of playful melodrama. "Don't even say it."

"Methinks the lady doth protest too much," Bobbie Ann teased.

"I think *you* doth lotht your mind." Jenny's face crinkled up as she laughed at her sister's notion. "Joe? Bobbie Ann, really now."

"Yes, really now."

Jenny's laughter turned to a petulant glare.

"Well, why not?" Bobbie Ann hoisted Danny higher on her hip, careful not to let him brush against the half-open door as she did. "You two sure made a darling couple tonight, standing with Cupid as a backdrop, in the light of a shower of fireworks, kissing."

"Kissing?" Jenny choked on the word, but she got it out, loud and clear.

Danny flinched.

Bobbie Ann placed a finger to her lips in warning.

Jenny glowered at her sister framed in the entryway of the home they'd grown up in. In a whisper forced through her teeth, Jenny insisted, "Joe and I were certainly *not* kissing."

"No? You sure looked awfully cozy up there."

"We did?" Jenny tried to swallow, but she couldn't seem to remember how.

"Uh-huh."

"Oh, Bobbie Ann, you don't think…that's not what other people will assume, is it? You don't suspect other people around town will think we were kissing, do you?"

"Well—"

"I stumbled! I *stumbled.*" Jenny stepped forward, her hand grasping at the rough edge of the door. Though she could not see anything but her sister and nephew in the small sliver of threshold, she looked in the direction of her front yard and the town that lay beyond it. "Do you think I could beat the gossip train if I ran outside right now and screamed at the top of my lungs, 'I stumbled into Joe Avery's arms. We were not kissing'?"

"Not a chance."

Jenny froze. Outside she heard the commotion of people on the sidewalks. Her neighbors, no doubt, returning from the festivities. She could just see them, carrying tired children in their arms, holding hands, polishing off the last wisp of pink cotton candy from a paper cone. She could just imagine what they were talking about too.

"Wasn't that a thrilling show?" someone would ask.

"The kind of thing you only fancy you'd see in a big city," someone else would reply.

"I never expected anything that flashy, that explosive, that bold, not here in our little town," a third would comment in hushed awe.

"No kidding!" the first speaker would chime in with vigor. "Who'd have ever thought you'd see the mayor making a fool of herself in the arms of the newspaper editor!"

Jenny put her hands to her cheeks and could feel the heat of her humiliation. She licked her lips and shook her head, repeating softly what her sister had just said. "Not a chance."

More noise drifted in from outside, drawing closer.

Bobbie Ann glanced over her shoulder, preoccupied even as she asked, "What, hon?"

"Not a chance," Jenny reprised. "That's going to be my motto where Joe and Alex are concerned. I have to forget love and romance, Bobbie Ann, and fix my sights on my work. I have too much to do and cannot let it be diminished by gossip or speculation, let alone the distraction of trying to enter a new relationship."

"With Joe or with Alex?"

"With either one." Jenny tugged her chin up and threw back her shoulders. "As far as I'm concerned, Joe Avery and Alex Michaels do not even exist as anything other than town doctor and newspaper editor. I will not give either one of them so much as another thought!"

"That may be harder than you think."

"Because this is such a small town?"

"That and because they are both coming up your walk right now."

"What?"

Bobbie Ann gave the door a shove. It slowly creaked and

swung open to reveal Alex and Joe making their way up the front walk, each with something in his hands, each trying to shoulder the other out of the way with every step.

"I believe this is my cue to skedaddle." Bobbie Ann clutched Danny tight, backed through the unlatched screen door, and let it fall shut with a *wham*.

On the porch, she gave Joe and Alex a brisk nod and never slowed as she hurried off, calling, "Nice to see you, gentlemen. Whatever happens tonight, at least I can rest assured there'll be a doctor on the scene and that I can read all about any criminal actions in a firsthand account in the paper."

"You should stay, Bobbie Ann. If the police don't need witnesses, I might!" Joe called after her as she swept a path between him and Michaels and went right on marching down the walkway.

"Can't. Have to put the munchkin to bed." Bobbie Ann lifted her dozing tot's hand to wave good-bye to them over her shoulder.

Fourth of July Delivers Biggest Spectacle Ever

—headline in the next edition of the Arrow

Seven

Joe smiled for no one but himself at the sweet sight of the little guy zonked out in Bobbie Ann's arms. It didn't take much imagination to picture the brunette walking away from him as Jenny and the little boy as—

"What are you two hound dogs doing here?" Jenny demanded.

Joe swung his gaze to the angry-faced mayor.

"Baying at the moon, for all the good it'll do them." Bobbie Ann cackled out a laugh.

Joe met Jenny's fiery eyes. He gave her a look that he hoped came off somewhere between predatory and playful and let out a long wolflike howl.

"Not funny."

"Your sister seemed to think so." They could hear Bobbie Ann giggling as she reached the end of the walk. Joe turned his upper body just enough to shout after her, "Tell Mark I said, 'Good luck tomorrow.'"

"Will do," she answered as she hurried off, out of the light from Jenny's porch.

"Good luck? Why are you wishing Mark good luck?" Jenny homed in on Joe, and he couldn't say he was disappointed to have her full attention, leaving Michaels standing there like a jerk. "Why would you tell Bobbie Ann to wish Mark good luck unless—you *know*, don't you?"

"Well, Your Honor, I know so much. You're going to have to narrow it down for me before I can give you an accurate answer."

Her usually bright eyes became slits. She cocked her head and her hair fell against her flushed cheek, tempting Joe to brush it away. "You know about Mark taking a job near Kansas City and that he, Bobbie Ann, and Danny are moving."

"They are? Jenny, that's terrific news." Alex did act on the impulse Joe had resisted, lurching forward to touch Jenny's face.

She did not bat the doctor's manicured hand away.

Joe stuffed his own hands in his jeans pockets and with them what he had brought to offer Jenny from the skirmish he and Michaels had just gone through.

"My sister is leaving, Alex. How could that possibly qualify as terrific news?" She frowned, and a little line creased her brow between her eyes.

Joe noticed this kind of thing about her more and more these days, as if since Michaels had arrived in town, he felt the need to keep an inventory of the way Jenny looked when she was mad, or confused, and especially when she was happy. He felt that anything he could discover about her, even the smallest nuance, might help him move into the lead over the doctor who seemed to have every advantage—money, looks, success, a cherished history with Jenny. Joe needed everything he had at his disposal to try to keep her from going back to Alex without even giving him a shot.

Michaels cleared his throat. "Jenny, I just meant—"

"And you!" She pointed her finger at the center of Joe's chest, cutting the doctor off without letting him explain.

"You knew about their plans to move and never said a word to me?"

"They asked me not to tell anyone." Joe shrugged.

"That's it?" She raised her eyebrows "That's all you have to say for yourself? No hemming? No hawing? No lengthy justification?"

"Nope." He shook his head. "Don't need one. I said I wouldn't tell and I didn't tell."

"But not even me? Not even knowing how much it would mean to me to know?"

"Not even then, Jenny. I gave my word, and that has to stand for something." Joe exhaled, suddenly keenly aware of the night air, the voices of townspeople still lingering in the street, and the two pairs of eyes fixed on him alone.

He raised his own eyes to meet the doctor's. Was the man thinking of all the things he'd told Joe while they sat in Doc Hobbs's office that first day? All the snide asides about Cupid's Corner replayed in Joe's thoughts along with Michaels's announcement that he planned to buy a house in Kansas City as soon as his summer obligation ended.

Joe turned to Jenny. How beautiful she looked, even with agitation coloring her expression. He'd give anything to find the way to win her hardened heart. He glanced over at Michaels again, his thoughts on the one secret that might bridge the gap between himself and Jenny. Well, he'd give almost anything to improve his odds, except his honor.

"I didn't tell you, Jenny," he said, his chest out and his hands still deep in his pockets. "Because I said I wouldn't, even though I probably could have used the news to get closer to you, to create a better connection between us. A man doesn't have much if he doesn't have his integrity."

"You're a little late, Avery. They've already finished

playing the patriotic music to accompany your heroic dissertation." Alex laughed, his eerily too-white teeth flashing.

Jenny opened her mouth.

Joe wondered if he just wished it or if her impatient look meant she intended to give her ex-fiancé grief over his idiotic remarks. He'd never know, because just then Alex stepped up, placing himself between Joe and Jenny.

"Here, Jenny, honey." Alex thrust out what he'd carried over from the flatbed truck. "You left this back at the town square."

"My…my hat!" Jenny snatched the hat, with its crushed crown, lopsided brim, and torn ribbon band with only a glob of clear glue where the big sunflower once had been. "What have you two done to my hat?"

"He did it," they both said at the same time, each of them jabbing an accusing thumb in the other's direction.

Only as Joe jerked his hand from his pocket to do it, a half-dozen delicate silk sunflower petals fluttered to the ground around his feet. Joe stared down at the telltale mess.

The straw hat rustled in Alex's hands.

Jenny seethed in silence.

"I'll buy you a new one," both Joe and Alex promised in unison.

"*I'll* buy her a new one," the doctor asserted through a clenched smile that bordered on maniacal.

"No, *I* will buy her the new hat," Joe countered. "You think because I don't pull down the kind of money a doctor does that I can't afford to—"

"Hush, both of you—and I mean *now!*"

They both zeroed their unwavering attention in on Jenny.

"Neither of you will buy me anything. Not now, not ever." She plunked her fists on her hips.

Joe stepped forward, nudging Alex aside as much as he could manage. "But I really would like to replace your hat, Jenny."

"Well, you can't. Even if I would accept a new hat from you, you can't replace mine because it was very special."

"Just looked to me like a straw hat with a tacky flower stuck on it, Jenny." Michaels examined the hat, sneered, then edged in front of Joe, slamming him in the midsection under the guise of handing him the hat. "I'm sure I could find you something far nicer in the city. In fact, you and I could drive in together, and we could pick you out the finest hat your heart desires. Then we could—"

"The hat my heart desires is the one you two clowns have torn apart. I know it wasn't much, but I bought it here in town, found the perfect sunflower and ribbon for it, and glued it on myself."

Joe fingered the rough underside of the rolled brim. He felt like a real heel for having been a part of tearing up something Jenny obviously cared about. He'd come here tonight acting like a big man, but now he felt two inches tall.

"Jenny, for what it's worth, I'm sorry about…this." Joe held up the sad thing.

"She doesn't want your apology, Avery," Michaels snapped.

"No, I don't." Jenny took a step back into the open doorway behind her.

Michaels began to follow her through the door as if he had the right.

Jenny stuck out her hand to stop him cold. "I don't want apologies or explanations. I don't want any visitors tonight or any other night, especially either of you. I don't want anything to do with you two except as far as I have to deal with you professionally."

"But, Jenny—" Joe stepped forward.

"I don't want to hear another word about it." She lifted one finger in warning as she backed across the threshold into her house. "What I do want is some peace and quiet. I want you two to act like grown men, if that's not asking too much. I want…I want my hat back the way it was! It was my signature hat in the mayoral race and I loved it. Now, thanks to you two, it's history. I wish I could say the same for this summer!"

The door slammed in their faces with a resounding *wham* that rivaled any of the thunderous firecrackers they'd heard this evening.

For one awkward minute they stood on the porch. Neither of them said a word. Neither of them moved.

Then Joe bent down and gathered up the petals strewn on the ground and tucked them back into his jeans pocket.

"Looks like we both lost this round, Avery." The doctor sighed and spun on the heel of his tasseled leather loafers.

"I wouldn't say that." Joe straightened up, putting him eye to eye with his romantic rival.

"No?" Michaels squinted, creating a cascade of furrows in the tanned skin around his eyes.

"Jenny mentioned history, which makes me think of that saying—those who do not learn from history are destined to repeat it."

"And?"

"And it doesn't look like Jenny has learned a thing about her history with you, so one can conclude…"

A slow, smarmy smile crept over the other man's mouth as he echoed, "One can only conclude…"

"That you are going to hurt her all over again if she gets involved with you, thinking you're going to settle down here and not want to go back to your life in the city." Joe gave the man an icy glare.

"Now, how's that going to happen?" Michaels gave a laugh that showed no trace of humor. "Didn't you hear the lady? She wants nothing to do with either one of us."

"You're not going to let that stand in the way of your trying to win her over again." Joe laughed too, a hard, short snort that spoke more of challenge than of chuckling. "I know it."

"And how do you know that?"

"Because Jenny Fox is worth fighting for—and trust me, you'll get a fight from me."

"I'm a healer, not a fighter, Avery." He held up his hands, walked past with a firm shove of his shoulder, then muttered, loud enough to make sure Joe heard him, "But you can flail away all you want, my friend. You still won't win her over."

"Maybe not." Joe turned, facing Dr. Michaels as the other man sauntered away. "I may not win her over, but get this perfectly clear, Michaels. I'll fight you with everything I can ethically use, because I will not stand by and let you hurt her ever again."

❦　❦

"Do you take this woman, and so on and so forth…"

"What are you doing here?" Jenny whispered so as not to draw the attention of the minister and the young couple standing at the front of the Cupid's Corner First Methodist Church.

"I'm here to take some wedding pictures." Joe swung a big black camera bag onto the last pew of the small, hushed church.

A week had passed since Jenny's run-in with Cupid and

Joe, which had resulted in the loss of her dignity and her favorite hat. She had thought she'd gotten over it, though not a soul in town seemed willing to let her forget it. However, seeing Joe in a public place for the first time since then churned up all the chagrin, irritation, and…other emotions that evening had caused.

Try as she might, she could not keep her agitated mood from coloring her tone as she gave him a cold once-over. "I thought that was Larry's job. And besides, aren't you supposed to take the pictures at the actual wedding, not the *rehearsal?*"

"Larry is taking pictures at the fund-raiser car wash at the high school." He tugged at the zipper on the leather bag so hard that it tore open with a metallic growl. The minister and the wedding couple stopped the run-through to turn and look back at them.

"Is there something I can help you with, Mr. Avery? Mayor Fox?" Reverend Edwards asked.

"Just here to take that photo for the paper, like I told the bride's mother I would." Joe pulled out a bulky black camera with a long strap and raised it up as if to prove the legitimacy of his story. "We're on a tight deadline and we can't get in my weekly multimarriage mania story this time if we wait until the actual ceremony tomorrow."

"Multimarriage mania story?" Jenny muttered under her breath, adding a huff that left no room for doubt that she didn't find the reference funny. She faced Reverend Edwards and the bride- and groom-to-be. "I just finished up the decorations for the Sunday School Teachers' Appreciation Banquet in the fellowship hall tonight and thought I'd peek in on the rehearsal before I left."

"Oh, the banquet!" Reverend Edwards, whom everyone

in town liked to call "a young Mr. Rogers-type, only not quite as flashy," was not known for his sharp memory. "That's tonight, isn't it?"

"Yes, it is," Jenny confirmed.

Joe stepped to the center of the aisle, crowding Jenny until she felt she either had to offer to focus the camera for him or get out of the way. "Excuse me, just trying to get off a good shot."

The camera flashed and then clicked as Joe advanced the film by hand.

Reverend Edwards made a quick check of his black plastic wristwatch, then looked at the couple before him with genuine regret. "I'm sorry we can't fiddle-faddle around any longer, you two. We need to hurry this along, even without the best man and matron of honor."

"But my sister and her husband are driving in from Tulsa, Reverend. They're just a little behind schedule." The bride glanced back at her mother, who sat perched in the front row, gripping the arm of the pew like a woman experiencing extreme turbulence on an airplane. "They'll be here soon, won't they, Mom?"

"Yes, I'm sure they will," Reverend Edwards spoke up before the mother could answer. "But I've got to get ready for this banquet. What time does it start, Mayor Fox?"

"In about forty minutes, Reverend."

Joe got off another shot with a brilliant flash.

"Oh, my." The minister blinked.

"That should do it for me. Thank you all." Joe gave a wave and took a step backward.

Jenny had to dodge to get out of his way. "Um, I need to get going too. Best wishes, you two," she called to the wedding couple.

The reverend blinked again, then looked at the bride, or in the general direction of the bride, either blinded by the flash or so distracted by his own tardiness that he could not focus. "You and your parents are welcome to stay here in the sanctuary to go over things for as long as you need to."

Satisfied that she had made the best good-bye she could, Jenny turned to go, but Joe's voice stopped her before she reached the door.

"Um, this banquet, are you going to go?"

Reverend Edwards continued to talk with the couple, his voice rumbling in the background. "You can show your sister and brother-in-law everything we've gone over so far."

Jenny thought about giving Joe a light, breezy reply as she swept out the door, but for some reason she couldn't do it. Something in the tentative way he asked her about the banquet compelled her to face him and explain. "No, I was just on the decorating committee. Bobbie Ann was supposed to go, but now that they're caught up with moving and all, she can't spare the time."

"There is one thing we do need to practice though. The part where, in my experience, nerves and the excitement of the day are most likely to cause a slip-up—the giving and receiving of the rings." It was a small sanctuary, and Reverend Edwards had a deceptively big voice that carried even to the very back with ease. "How I do wish you had someone here who could walk you through that just once, so I'd feel confident you know how to proceed with that part of the ceremony."

"So, you're not going." Joe put the camera away but stayed bent over the bag, his fingers toying with a second zippered pouch. "Because, the thing is, if you *were* going I had something I wanted to…"

Jenny tensed, unsure of what he was getting at but aware

of her promise to keep her distance from this man, despite her sister's urgings to the contrary.

"That is, I thought you might want to..."

"Say, I think I have the perfect solution!" The minister clapped his hands together, startling everyone present. "Mayor Fox? Mr. Avery?"

Jenny and Joe exchanged anxious looks.

"Why don't you two come here and stand in for the best man and matron of honor?" The minister motioned for them to come to the altar.

"Us? There?" Jenny pointed. Her pulse raced, and she glanced around like a trapped animal looking for a means of escape.

"Oh, do it, Mayor Fox, please." The bride's mother stood, color finally rushing back into her face. "And if Mr. Avery will let me, I can snap off a few photos of you two standing in. My neighbor, Elsie Horner, will turn green with envy when she sees in the paper that the mayor and the *Arrow*'s editor stood in at my little girl's rehearsal.

"Not that I want to inspire envy, Reverend," she quickly added over her shoulder to her minister, even as she rushed down the aisle to claim Joe's camera. "It's just that ever since Elsie's daughter got a congratulatory letter from the governor for winning the spelling bee, I haven't heard the end of it."

"B-but I can't be in the paper looking like this." It was a lousy excuse for avoiding standing in a wedding party at the church altar with Joe Avery, but Jenny couldn't think of anything better under the circumstances. "I've been decorating all afternoon. My jeans are filthy."

"Oh, honey, Mr. Avery is a wonder at fixing those kinds of things, I'm sure. He can crop off that picture so no one sees your jeans at all." The bride's mother hurried past. "Isn't that right, Mr. Avery?"

Joe mumbled something, his attention on the camera bag.

"But my hair…it's awful. Even Mr. Avery can't very well crop my hair out of the picture, now can he?"

"No, but I can give you this to cover it up a little."

Jenny felt Joe move in behind her. Something scratched her arm. She looked first at him and the entirely guileless expression in those big brown eyes. She caught her breath, then dropped her gaze to his offering.

"My hat!" She was so excited to see her old favorite that she almost squeezed it to her chest in a hug. Luckily, she recognized before she did it, that that would only ruin what at first inspection looked like an almost perfect repair job. "If it wasn't for the patch in the brim and these little globs of glue on some of the flower petals, I'd swear it was brand-new."

"Yeah, sorry about those globs. I never handled a hot glue gun before. Pritchy tried to explain to me how to use the one she loaned me, but I never quite got the hang of it." He held up his hand to reveal small but angry blisters on two of his fingers.

That sight touched her as much or more than the gift itself. "Oh, Joe, you burned yourself trying to fix my hat?"

"Just a little. It's nothing, really."

It's not nothing, she wanted to say. It's something. Something special. It tells me about what kind of man you are, it tells me that you respect the things I value, even if you can't immediately see the value in them yourself. It tells me you're nothing like Alex Michaels. She wanted to say all those things, but how could she, really? Standing in the sanctuary of her church, with people watching them both, watching her, waiting. Waiting! That thought snapped her out of her sentimental musings.

"Will you stand in and let me get the picture for the

paper, Mayor Fox?" The bride's mother gave a pleading look. "Please?"

"Well, I guess if they can crop out my dirty jeans and I can hide my ratty hair under my hat—"

Before she could finish her sentence, Joe lightly slid the hat from her hands and placed it on her head.

He offered her his arm. "Shall we?"

The trip down that aisle was one of the longest walks she'd ever taken. And as Reverend Edwards went over the details of how the bride and groom would exchange rings tomorrow when they took their vows, Jenny couldn't help but sneak a look at Joe.

While she could not let herself dwell on the strange feeling of standing up here with Joe so near, there was one thing she could not deny. She had a whole new level of regard for this outsider with his tenacity, his gentle teasing, and his own kind of honor. Joe had fixed her hat and with that simple act had repaired at least a little of her battered faith in the male segment of mankind.

From This Day Forward

For better or worse, Cupid's Corner has reached the midpoint in the 58-day attempt to break the town's longstanding record for the most marriages in one summer.

Local residents joined eloping couple Cheri Pfeiffer and Richard Shepherd, of Miami, Oklahoma, in the celebration of their marriage, the 35th performed in town since the July 4 kickoff of the event. Mayor Jenny Fox presided over a gala to mark the occasion, in which she also unveiled a billboard designed by the high school industrial arts program. The large painted sign features a wedding chapel with a wooden cutout of a bride and groom that can be moved farther down the aisle each time another couple marries in our town.

"We are proud to have this billboard as a delightful addition to our festivities and look forward to the day when we reach our goal," Mayor Fox told the crowd of approximately 100 people. The billboard was paid for with monies raised in part by the Mighty Archers Pep Squad in conjunction with the We-Do Weddings Chapel and the To Have and To Hold Self-Storage Units on East Main.

—newspaper article in the
Cupid's Corner Weekly News Arrow, *page four*

Eight

"O kay, where is he?" Jenny slammed her copy of the *Arrow* down on the countertop of the newspaper's front office. She stretched up on tiptoe and pressed her belly to the high-gloss vanilla white surface to lean over far enough to peer into the doorway behind the long counter.

If she could, she'd march right back there and grab Joe Avery by the shirt collar herself. However, since the arrival of the new editor, the paper had expanded to take over the empty dry-cleaner's building next door to its longtime location. This meant no one could get back into the work stations unless they were let through a locked side door by someone, usually a high-school journalism student working as an intern/receptionist for the semester or summer.

This only added to Jenny's frustration and her more-surly-than-serene mood. She pounded on the countertop again, the paper rustling in her hand. "Where is he? Where's that mangy excuse for an editor who put *my* picture and story about the wed-a-thon on page four? Page four! Next to the livestock report!"

Chairs scraped over the hardwood floors of the back offices. She heard the murmur of voices and then a hoot of

125

laughter that Jenny recognized as coming from the head of the advertising department. Somewhere beyond the narrow open doorway a radio blared out a chart-topping country song. A phone rang and rang and rang. No one answered it. No one came forward to attend to her demands, least of all the culprit responsible for her wrath.

"I know you're in there, Joe Avery. I asked around and everyone said they saw you duck inside the newspaper office—or should I say slink inside the back door?—when you found out I was looking for you." *Everyone* in this case consisted of Nurse Pritchet and Alex, who had been at the café where Jenny always went to eat lunch and read her edition of the *Arrow* hot off the presses.

Apparently Joe had been there too, as he usually was on the days Jenny routinely ate there, but he hadn't stayed long once he'd learned how truly unhappy she was with his handling of the halfway point in the wed-a-thon.

"Joe? Would you get yourself out here? I have a few things to say to you."

The phone stopped ringing. The country song ended, and an ad for a car dealership came on. The fluorescent lights buzzed overhead.

Jenny folded her arms across her chest. To treat her story like this was one thing, but then to ignore her, hiding in his office like some coward—she'd never have expected it of Joe.

"It just goes to show you. You think you know a person," she grumbled between clenched teeth. She unfolded the newspaper on the glass countertop. Carefully, she smoothed the page open so she could see both the story Joe had written and the picture he'd run—of her placing the bride-and-groom marker even with the pew marked with the number thirty-five. Try as she might to guard against it, some of her initial anger ebbed as she studied the grainy black-and-white photo.

With one finger she traced the outline of her favorite straw hat. She lowered her head, narrowing her eyes to better make out the image of the mended straw with a brand-new ribbon for a band sporting a big silk sunflower, glued back in place petal by petal. She shook her head, her hair dragging back and forth slowly over the denim bodice of her dress. She tried not to let the sentimentality get the better of her rightful irritation with Joe, but when she looked again at the picture, she couldn't help herself.

She still recalled the hopeful expression on Joe's face when he'd given her back the hat he'd repaired all by himself. She sighed, and this time wonder and a kind of humble admiration colored her softly spoken words when she said, "You think you know a person…"

"Hey! There you are!" The heavy glass-paneled door whooshed open, ushering in a gust of wind that flapped the stack of pink phone-message papers anchored on the counter with a rock. Joe strode into the front office as if he owned the place—and everything in it.

Well, he didn't own her. In fact, he didn't own the paper either; he was just in charge of it. But he wasn't in charge of her, and if he thought he could take control away from her in this matter, she would show him differently with one icy hard glare. She crossed her arms and turned slowly on her heel.

The sunlight streaming in from the large plate-glass windows behind him highlighted the man's broad shoulders and glinted off his inky black hair. He rolled his shirt sleeve back another turn, then pushed the soft blue fabric to the bend of his elbow.

"I heard a rumor that you're running all over town shouting out how much you need me and how you want to get your hands on me, Mayor." He grinned at her.

Jenny's stomach lurched in the kind of exhilarating way it would while riding a wild roller coaster. It was the grin that did it, she thought, trying not to look directly at the proprietary smile she'd never seen him give anyone else. Lucky for her she was immune to any long-term side effects.

"And I heard a rumor that you ran back to hide in your office rather than deal with my reaction to this." She held up the page she'd been studying with all the flair of a TV lawyer pulling out the conclusive piece of evidence at the climax of a murder trial.

Joe cocked his head to the right and then to the left, his hand stroking his chin like a man giving something due consideration. "What's the matter?" he finally asked. "Did you take umbrage with the livestock report?"

"I could care less about the livestock report." She jabbed one finger into the story. "I took umbrage with this."

"What? You don't like the picture?"

Jenny's jaw locked up so tight she thought Joe probably heard her back teeth squawk under the pressure. Still, she succeeded in grinding out a reproof. "There are so many things about this that I don't like, I don't even know where to begin to tell you about them."

Joe swept one hand out, his mouth open to speak.

Jenny never gave him the chance. "I take that back. I do know where to begin—page four. How about we begin with page four?" She rattled the paper clutched in her hand in his direction. "Let's begin there, shall we?"

"I have a better idea. Let's begin…" He paused, lifted a finger to tell her to bear with him a minute, then stuck his hand in his jeans pocket. His dark gaze never wavered from her face, and the sly tilt of his lips only took on a more rakish angle as he foraged for whatever it was he was trying to retrieve. It took a tug or two, but finally, he fished out a set of four or five keys attached to a keychain in the shape of a large number one.

The bright red plastic tag, a promotional giveaway from the paper's largest advertiser, wasn't practical. It had too many corners to make it easy to pull from a pocket. That Joe used it anyway told Jenny a lot about him—he had a good heart, and a very good head for business. The rest of him wasn't a torture to look at either, she thought, then gasped at her own wayward observation.

If Joe noticed anything amiss, he didn't show it. He merely jangled the keys in front of her and said, "Let's begin by going back into my office where we can have some privacy."

Jenny's hand contracted, crumpling the newspaper in her grasp. Unnerved by the unwitting act, she tucked her hand behind her back. "I…um…I, that is, no. No, thank you, Joe. I, um, hardly think that will be necessary. This is a public matter, and since I am acting as a public official, it can certainly be discussed *publicly*."

"Aw. That's too bad." He feigned a pout and slid the keys back into his pocket, leaning toward her with his upper body as he winked and whispered, "I was looking forward to a little time alone with you, even if it was strictly business."

"Thanks, but no thanks, you've already given me the business with that sorry excuse for publicity." She threw the paper down on the counter. "Now I'll be happy to give you a piece of my mind—"

"Can I get you a cup of coffee first?" He strode past her and slapped his palms on the countertop.

Whether he planned to leap over the counter or just to lean over and call out to someone to bring the coffee, Jenny did not wait to see.

"Oh no, you don't." She lunged forward, nabbing him by the back of his shirt.

He flailed his arms much more than her grabbing him warranted.

Jenny rolled her eyes at his corny antics, giving the fabric pinched between her thumb and finger a shake just for good measure. "You can't get away from me that easily, Joe. Now that I've got you, I won't let you run off until *I'm* ready to turn you loose."

"You have no idea how long I've waited for you to say that." He turned around slowly, his hands held up in surrender. "I'm all yours, sugarlips."

Jenny released his shirt faster than if it had been a hot coal. "Don't you dare call me *sugarlips.* "

"You'd prefer *honeymuffin?*"

She felt the heat of her anger and embarrassment flood her cheeks. A few choice responses swirled through her mind, but she held them all back, forcing herself to bring this idiotic exchange back to the thing that brought her here in the first place. "What I prefer is that when something regarding the town's welfare takes place, it get front-page coverage in our one and only town newspaper."

"Unveiling a billboard with a movable bride and groom is a matter regarding the town's welfare?" He scratched his head.

She didn't buy the confused act for one moment. "That we are ahead of our goal on the record-breaking wed-a-thon is the news here, Mr. Editor, and if you don't know that, then—"

"I covered the story, Jenny." His expression went cold, his tone low, like the threatening rumble of distant thunder.

"With a smart-alecky opening like 'for better or worse,'" she shot back.

"Just doing my part to keep up with the whole everything-has-to-have-a-wedding-theme theme." He crossed his arms. "I got all the pertinent information in there, spelled all the names of the businesses right. What more did you want?"

"I want it not to be buried on page four."

"That's not your call."

"As mayor of this town, I—"

"Mayor-schmayor. That dog don't hunt here, Your Honor." He wrung the term he liked to use to annoy her through a joyless smile.

"Oh, you've made it perfectly clear what you think of my ideas as mayor. You've opposed this whole PR opportunity from the very beginning—"

"It has nothing to do with your ideas or your precious publicity stunt. This has to do with who *I* am and what *I* do. What I do is run the newspaper. This is the press, the fourth estate—protected by a nifty constitutional amendment you may have heard of." He scowled. "Even in a town as small and idyllic as this one, we do not take orders from local politicians on how to cover stories, what to print, or where to put them in the layout."

He had a point, but she couldn't bring herself to concede with anything more than a tight-lipped *harrumph*.

"The truth is, Jenny, I don't for one second believe that's what you want to do here. I don't think you're trying to flex your political muscles to coerce the paper into being your mouthpiece."

"Political muscles? Coercion? Mouthpiece? My, you make it all sound so…" She feigned a shudder, then realized the action aptly portrayed her opinion of the things Joe was suggesting. She never had any motivation as bleak as those. "I only wanted a little cooperation, Joe, a little kindness toward my cause. I thought that despite our differences, you might have some genuine concern for the town and want—"

"I have plenty of genuine concern for this town, Jenny.

It's my home. And I plan on making it my home for a long time to come."

"Sure." She sniffed and shifted her weight from one hip to the other. "A long time in city time, no doubt."

"City time? What are you talking about?"

"City time—it's very different from time in a place like Cupid's Corner, and you know it. In a city, if someone has to wait that long" —she snapped her fingers— "after the light turns green, horns start honking. But here, if someone takes their time getting going at a green light, we—"

"We call Sheriff Hadley to come and haul them off to the city for observation," he concluded for her. "Because Cupid's Corner doesn't have any red lights or green lights, Jenny, just the few yellow flashing ones."

"I was speaking in metaphors, and you know it."

"Sorry, I didn't have my English-to-metaphor dictionary handy." He grinned. "Or should I make that my country-talk to city-talk dictionary?"

She raised her eyebrows. "If only there were such a thing. It might have come in awfully handy a few times since you arrived for your little sabbatical in town."

"Sabbatical? I think you have me confused with a certain doctor. He's the one just around for the summer. I'm the one that's moved here to stay." He jabbed his thumb to the center of his chest.

"Alex is *from* here. It's different." Jenny hadn't meant to voice any of these things, but now that she heard them aloud, she couldn't emphasize them enough for the arrogant outsider. "If *Alex* had been the one running the paper, *he'd* have understood the importance of—"

"Hold it right there." He shut his eyes as if he had to cut off any other sensory information just to take in what she had said. "That's what all this is about, isn't it?"

"What? What all *what* is about?" Jenny shook her head, though she knew he couldn't see it. When he did open his eyes again, she tipped her head to one side and gave him a teasing smile—the kind that, if it came from him, she would have called a smirk. "Maybe it's time for one of those translating dictionaries—Joe-talk to plain-talk."

"Oh, I'll give you plain-talk, Your Honor. You may not like what you hear, but I'll give it to you real plain." He stepped close enough that she could actually feel the rise and fall of his chest. "All this, the source of all your problems with me—from your resentment of my participation in the town council meeting, my very presence there, to your refusal to even consider going out with me, to your aggravation over how I covered this story, it all stems from one thing, doesn't it?"

"Well, yeah." She blinked. "I guess you could say that. It all comes from you. That is the common denominator in every one of those cases. Our schools may not be as fancy and forward thinking as those in the big cities, but they do teach us about things like common denominators, you know."

"There it is."

"There *what* is?" She hunched her shoulders up in exasperation. The movement brought her just far enough away from Joe that she no longer felt the heat from his body. This both relieved and disappointed her at the same time, which only made her scrunch her back up more and wind her arms more closely to her body.

"There is the true common denominator, Jenny—the way you choose to look at me."

She jerked her head up, wondering if he knew what she had been thinking.

"You see me, and consequently you always treat me, as

an outsider. Someone who does not belong here. Someone who, if given the chance, would walk off in a heartbeat and leave this place—and anybody who chose to remain here—to race back to my life in the city."

"I most certainly do—" She stopped herself. Did she? Was that a factor? "No. I don't accept your assessment. If you and I have our differences, it's because we're...different."

"That can be a good thing, you know." He put his hand on her upper arm and moved in close enough to flutter the hair tucked behind her ear as he whispered, "They say opposites attract. We're just doing what they tell us we should be doing."

Jenny bristled, but she did not move away. Chin high, she carried off a very difficult mix of irritation and good humor as she suggested, "If *they* told you to go jump off Graffiti Bridge, would you do that? Please? I'll even put aside my differences with you and help you with the first step."

" 'Mayor Launches Editor Off Route 66 Landmark.' Now *there's* front-page news for you."

"Front-page news." Jenny tossed her head back and groaned. "Arrgh. Thanks for reminding me why I came in here in the first place."

"Jenny, sweet as the billboard story was and adorable as you looked hiking the happy couple up the aisle toward your goal—"

"It's not my goal; it's for the whole town."

"Fine. As adorable as you looked hiking the happy couple up toward the *town's* goal, we are a month into this thing with a month more to go—every little benchmark simply cannot be front-page fodder. Other things happen. Other things affect the people here."

"I know other things affect people here, Joe." She pivoted on her heel with a vengeance, spurred by the sheer arrogance of his remark. As if only he was privy to the underlying needs and concerns of the people she had known and loved all her life. "Do you honestly think I don't know that?"

He straightened but did not back down an inch. "Sometimes you don't act like it, if I may say so, Your Honor. Focusing far too much energy on a...on a wed-a-thon?"

Heat rose from her chest to her neck and into the hollows of her cheeks like steam to signal she had finally reached her boiling point. Fists at her sides, she glared at Joe, practically nose to nose with the know-it-all editor. "Do you think I'd be trying a desperate publicity grab like a wed-a-thon if I weren't concerned about the deeper problems that affect the citizens of my town? Do you think I don't lie awake nights worrying over what will become of this place if we don't turn things around soon? That I don't feel just a little more panicked every time someone like Alex or my sister moves away?"

"Whoa. Whoa." He held both hands up, then grabbed her lightly by the shoulders and gave a little shake. "Slow down there. I never said you didn't care about this town. I would never say that. It's just that sometimes you don't act like you can separate the real needs of the town and this pet project of yours. Sometimes your perspective regarding this publicity event gets out of whack. That's all I'm saying."

Jenny bit her lower lip. She tried to think of some clever, cutting way to deny Joe's accusation, but none came. None came because he was right. That did not make it any easier for her to look him in the eye and still feel good about herself. So she did the only other thing that came to mind. She burst into tears.

❧ ❧

"I didn't know where else to bring her. She wouldn't go back to her office because she didn't want anyone to see her so overwrought. Obviously, I couldn't parade her over to the café for the same reason." Joe sighed and leaned one elbow on the clinic's counter, peering in at Pritchy through the open glass panel. "Since Bobbie Ann and Mark moved last week, there wasn't a family member to call and ask what to do. Jenny wouldn't let me take her home—said it would cause people to talk, the two of us seen going into her house in the middle of the day."

"She's right. It's a very small town, Joseph. People *do* talk." Pritchy did not even look up from the magazine she was reading.

"People in cities talk too, you know," he muttered. Sure, it came out defensive. He felt defensive, especially after the startling revelation he'd just had that so much of his trouble with Jenny originated from his status as an outsider. To her, he'd always be someone who did not belong, who did not have roots here, who could pick up and leave at any minute. No wonder she would not risk involvement with him. No wonder she distrusted his judgment about the town's future. She saw him as a man who had no real stake in that future or in anyone who planned to make this town their home forever.

She was wrong about him in that matter. Not only had he been small-town raised, but he'd even spent much of his early childhood in Texas, Oklahoma, and Missouri, in places not all that different from her hometown. Of course, how could she know that about him when she became so flighty around him, or why they became so focused on their divergent businesses that they had little time to talk about personal things, much less childhood memories?

To be fair, though, he could see her point of view to some extent. He could certainly see how someone so hurt by people leaving the place she loved might feel gun-shy of newcomers. "But it's not like people who live in cities are heartless, you know. It's not like we don't care about each other, about our neighbors. It's not like having been born and raised someplace else besides Cupid's Corner makes you unable to appreciate the subtle nuances, pitfalls, and values of the quiet life here."

"What are you prattling on about, Joseph?" Pritchy's head bobbed up, frown lines framing her pink-lipsticked mouth.

"I was just saying that…" He cleared his throat. "Um, so, do you think I did the right thing in bringing Jenny here to the clinic?"

"Yes. You did fine. It's quiet here. She needs some quiet. Been working her fingers to the bone, poor thing."

"Yeah, that's true. She has." Joe scrubbed his short fingernails over his scalp, not caring whether it would leave his hair standing up at odd angles. Who did he have to impress here at the clinic anyway? Doc Local-Boy was off doing good deeds, health screenings at the senior center. Nothing impressed or surprised Pritchy—she'd seen everyone in town at their worst at one point or another—and Jenny… As far as he knew, Jenny was conked out cold, napping on the couch in Doc's office.

"Do you think she's okay? I mean, really okay? Not just right now but…you know?" He did not want to say he thought she was stretched too thin, but that's what he thought. He did not want to imply he thought she might need more than a nap in a quiet spot to cure her anxieties, but he thought that, too. He only wished he knew what more he could do to help her. Secretly, he hoped that if he hinted around long enough, good ol' Pritchy would come through with some kind of answer for him. "I'm worried about her, Pritchy. Because one minute everything was just business as usual between us—we were arguing over her pointless publicity event—then she just suddenly burst out crying. Just like that, for no reason at all."

"She'll be fine. She just needs some rest."

Joe glanced from the nurse sitting behind the tall counter in the receptionist area to the closed door that led to the room where Jenny had gone to lie down.

"Don't you even think of going back there and pestering her," Pritchy warned. "She needs her rest."

"And what will have changed when she wakes up? Everything that made her tell me to go jump off Graffiti Bridge—it will still be here, waiting for her."

"She told you to jump off Graffiti Bridge?" Finally something got through enough to make the older woman look up, this time with a devilish glint in her eyes. "What did you do to deserve that?"

He slouched his shoulders like a kid confessing some misdeed to the teacher. "I didn't make a front-page story out of the billboard dedication and the fact that they're more than halfway to their goal."

Pritchy clucked her tongue and shook her head. "Don't you know that you catch more flies with honey than you do with vinegar, son?"

"I cannot use the newspaper as the mayor's public bulletin board, Pritchy. It goes against my ethics as a journalist. I also won't use my power and position to place stories so that I can personally score points with Jenny either."

"Well, of course not, but there are people besides Jenny

who honestly believed that story warranted a spot on the front page."

"What does that mean?"

"It means that maybe you should examine your own motivations."

"My motivation is to do my job. I've done a big story on the wed-a-thon or something related to all the summer events every week so far. They can't all be front page."

"She's just looking for a little local support. She needs to find a way to keep folks' interest up for the long haul." Pritchy arched one darkly lined brow.

"There have to be other ways for her to revitalize the project." He moved to the closed door and pushed it open just enough to let him see down the hallway to Doc's office, where Jenny had disappeared earlier. "Just like there've got to be other ways for me to help her besides compromising my professional integrity."

"If you want to help her, let her rest." The wheels on Pritchy's chair squealed as she pushed herself back enough to confront Joe in the doorway.

"A twenty-minute nap is not going to give her the kind of distance she needs to regain her perspective, and you know it."

"Then give her thirty minutes," Pritchy muttered. "Give her an hour or two. Give her a whole day, for that matter."

An hour, a day, he'd gladly give that much time to Jenny, if he could spend it with her. What good would it do him, though, if they spent that time in a place where she would be the insider and he, some kind of interloper? If only there were a way to give her that distance to restore her perspective, to find a place where neither one of them was the insider.

Joe's head jerked up. "Pritchy, that's it! You've got it!"

"I do?"

"It's perfect! I can't believe I never thought of it before."

"Never thought of what before?"

He stepped back and let the door fall shut. With a quick salute to the nurse as he headed for the front door, he called out, "When Jenny wakes up, tell her I went to do some research. Tell her if she drops by the *Arrow* to see me later today, she won't regret it. I've got a plan that will accomplish goals for both of us—save my integrity, solve her publicity problem, fulfill my desire to help her out, and meet her need to step back and get the big picture…"

"Is that *all?*" Pritchy laughed at the monumental agenda he'd just proposed.

"Actually, no. If this plan works, it might finally give me the edge over young Doctor Past-Love and open up the door for Jenny and me to finally start our relationship on an equal and fair footing."

Get Your Ads in Now!
The Cupid's Corner Weekly News Arrow
is now taking advertisements
for a special free supplement to be
distributed with the paper and separately
in tourist stops, restaurants, and towns
along nearby stretches of old Route 66.
Don't Delay!
Space is limited
and
Time is running out.
Call the Arrow's advertising department today!

—flier ad copy given to all local businesses in
Cupid's Corner and the surrounding area

Nine

W ell?"
      Time is running out. Call the Arrow's *advertising department today!* Jenny finished reading the simple mailer in her hand, then looked back to Joe.

She'd awakened from her nap only a few minutes ago and come roaring out of Doc's office, all flustered and light-headed just thinking of the scene she'd made and the time she'd lost today already. Obviously she had needed the respite. She had not experienced a truly restful night's sleep all summer and had let herself get so tired she showed little or no judgment in dealing with Joe and the whole newspaper incident. That, however, hardly justified sleeping on the job!

So naturally, when she awoke and got her bearings enough to realize where she was and how late it had become, she dashed into the waiting room ready to head straight back to her office. Not six feet before she reached the outside door, who should come strolling in to intercept her but Joe, clutching something he thought she absolutely had to see.

"Well? What do you think?" Joe prompted again. "Knowing you, I figured you'd never come over to my office today, feeling you had to get back to work, so I made a special trip over here to show this to you."

Jenny scrubbed at her forehead as though that might stimulate her brain to think how best to handle this new situation. Still, she had no idea what he expected of her, so she grimaced, shrugged, handed the slip of white paper back to him, and said the only thing that sprang to mind. "Um, everything is spelled right?"

"No, no, I wasn't giving it to you to proofread. I want to know what you think." Joe pushed the paper back toward her, beaming like a kid showing off a straight A report card.

"It's, um, very neatly done." She shoved at his arm, refusing to accept the page from him.

"Yeah, well, I've managed to get a few things printed up legibly in my time." He glowered at her, but the harshness quickly dissipated, and that hopeful puppy-dog look returned.

How could one look from this man—this man whom she definitely was not interested in—turn her ironclad resolve to absolute mush? Countless times she had sworn she would not let him get to her, not let him make her laugh or make her feel all warm and woozy inside. Yet when he gave her that your-opinion-matters-to me look, she wanted to smile and give it right back at him.

"And?" He gave the page a shake to urge her answer along.

"And…" She hoped the keen-eyed newspaperman in him did not notice how just the accidental touch of his hand on hers made her shiver as she finally took the mailer from him. She told herself she was still unsteady from her work-weary lapse into tears. "And…"

She could feel him watching her, actually feel how pleased he was with what he had done. A month ago she might have looked for any reason to do just the opposite—to find fault with anything Joe Avery presented her with, especially if it had any connection to her project. Now all she could think of was that he'd mended her favorite hat and then today he'd so sweetly protected her from humiliation when she'd acted like a big baby in his office.

Who else would have spirited her off to just the right place, the clinic, knowing no one would be there but Nurse Pritchet to see her fall apart? Who else would have left her to nap on the couch for more than an hour without sauntering down to the café to get a few free cups of coffee out of the wild tale of her antics? Who else would have returned, waited for her to wake up so he could make sure she felt better, then presented her with something he thought would "improve her mood immensely and make up for his inability to keep the story on page one all summer," as Joe had put it? The answer came clear and swift to her mind. No one. No one else would have done that for her.

Everyone else around here, everyone who had known her all her life, would have expected her to pull herself together—to snap out of it on the spot and get back to her responsibilities. Jenny sighed. Only Joe would think to treat her so tenderly.

That's why she had to do everything in her power to keep herself from caring about the man.

If she let herself, she could get awfully attached to Joe. Then where would she be when he decided to move up the career ladder by moving to some larger city? Joe was young and good at what he did. Anyone could see that small-town newspaper editor was neither the most glamorous nor the most exciting job a man with Joe's talent and experience could aspire to. No doubt the time would come when he would want advancement. Since he came into his job with the *Arrow* at the top, his only option to move up would be to move away.

It had been easy enough for Alex to leave town, despite so many things that should have compelled him to stay. Leaving would be no problem for a man like Joe. How could it be? What did he have here to tie him? Even a relationship that promised long-term commitment, a home, and a family would not be enough to keep a man here if he really wanted to get out. Jenny had learned that lesson the hard way once. She had no intention of repeating her past mistakes.

"And…" She forced her gaze to the heavy black words before her. She supposed she should be gentle, considering how nice Joe had been to her today, but her disquieted emotions would not cooperate. She could all but feel the wall go up inside her and lock into place. She had to keep herself at all costs from doing anything that might encourage Joe. She could not give him cause to hope that they would ever be more than two people whose jobs required they work together. "I have no idea what you want to hear from me about this flier, Joe. It looks fine. Now, if you don't mind, I've been away from my office long enough."

"Fine? That's all you have to say?" He caught her by the crook of her elbow and kept her from scurrying off as she'd planned.

Jenny froze, still keenly aware of the clinic door and her escape beyond it. She felt unable to walk away from Joe—because of his news, not his commanding presence or the touch of his hand on her arm, she hurried to remind herself. The afternoon sunlight warmed her back as he turned her away from the nearby windows. At least, she blamed the sun for the rising temperature under her collar—the sun and her spiking irritation at Joe's attempts to delay her.

"This morning you pitched a fit in the front office of the paper for more publicity because you didn't think we'd done enough to support your pet project, Jenny." He flexed his fingers gently, adjusting his hold so that it restricted but in no way hurt her. "Now I show you what could well represent the solution to that and your lagging publicity problems, and all you can say is 'fine'?"

"The solution? To what?" She narrowed her eyes in a show of suspicion, knowing it would also conceal any reaction she might have standing so close to this man. "Are you saying that this supplement will be in some way connected to the wed-a-thon and the attempt to break the previous Hitchin' City record?"

"That's exactly what I'm saying, Your Honor."

"Okay, that got my attention," she confessed. "You have five minutes to explain this to me, so don't play coy."

"Me? Coy?" He batted his thick black eyelashes in mock coquettish style.

Though she battled against it, a small sputter of laughter bubbled through Jenny's tightly sealed lips before she issued a sterner warning. "Time's awastin', Joe."

"Yes ma'am." He gave a sharp salute. The paper crackled as he took it from her hand. "The first thing you should know is that I've talked to the staff, and they liked the idea very much. Also, because we'll use appropriate stories from the archives, plenty of photos from past issues as well as current ones, and as many ads as we can patchwork in there, we can pull it all together really quickly. We'll have it done in plenty of time to have it circulating a good two weeks before Labor Day. It's all right here."

"Where?" She studied the flier he offered up as proof.

"Well, it's…" He glanced down at the advertising, then sucked in his breath, a blend of wincing and caution in his expression. "Okay, it's not exactly there, but when the salespeople make the presentation, that will all be clear. Believe me, I've worked up one terrific sales pitch for this."

"Why does the way you look at me when you say that give me a funny knotting sensation in my stomach?" she asked.

"Because you can barely contain the building thrill of sweet anticipation for what's to come?" He grinned.

"Could be," she droned. "But just in case it's not that, why don't you astound me with an alternative possibility?"

He leaned in until the tip of his nose almost touched hers, so close she could see the flicker of amusement in his eyes as he spoke in a low, hurried murmur. "How about, you're sublimating your feelings of intense attraction for me, and it's manifesting itself in the form of physical discomfort, centered in your digestive tract, particularly in the stomach region."

"Nope." She said it with unwavering conviction. However, deep down she did not reject his idea so easily.

"You sure that's not it?"

She clenched her jaw, inhaled sharply, and said nothing.

Joe raised his hands in a gesture of surrender. "I don't know what it is then. Maybe you're hungry. What say I take you over to the café and get you something to eat?"

"What say you cut to the chase? Tell me what I need to know about this newspaper supplement of yours so I can get back to my office and back to work." *And away from you,* she wanted to tack on but did not dare. Another time she might have gotten off the zinger without missing a beat, but today things seemed far too close to the surface.

"The chase?" He cleared his throat, but that did not dissipate the air of uneasiness that surrounded him, from his posture to the rasp in his voice. He glanced around them, lingering a moment over the frosted glass that separated them from Nurse Pritchet's prying eyes. "Um, maybe that's something best talked about somewhere else. If you have to get back to your office, I'll walk you back. We can talk there, or maybe get together later, if you want."

What she wanted now was to put some distance between herself and Joe. The last thing she needed at this point was another second in his company, much less a drawn-out conversation. The more time they spent together, the more he would hope she might relent and go out with him—and the more she thought she might do just that. But in the end, what would be the point? It just would not be fair to either of them. She had to do whatever it took to make sure they stayed apart as much as possible.

"The facts, Joe. Get to the facts." She pressed her fingers into the corners of her eyes. "So we can get this over with and go our separate ways."

"Right. The facts." He laced his long fingers together and stretched out his arms like a virtuoso preparing for a difficult piano concert.

If that was supposed to demonstrate to her how casually he approached this exchange, it did not work. "Out with it, Joe. You now only have four minutes."

"I don't even need that much time." He waved his hand in the air. He sighed and then his words rushed out, firm but fast in a concise patter that automatically made her anxious. "The facts are that in order to do this and do it right, we need some good old-fashioned legwork. I just don't have the kind of time it would usually take to get a publicity tabloid of this nature into the locales where it would do the most good without actually going out and doing a lot of the placement in person."

"Why, Joe, I'm surprised—pleasantly, of course—that you'd offer to do that, given how you've felt about this project all along." She stuck out her hand to shake on the contribution he proposed, to let him know she would not be hoodwinked into anything less than he had just offered and to show her gratitude for it. "Thank you. Thank you very much."

Joe ignored her gushing and crossed his arms to rebuff her gesture. "I have to say I'm pretty surprised myself."

"At what?" She let her hand fall to her side, alert to the possibility that he was up to something.

"That you expect me to run around acting like your errand boy on this thing." The set of his face went grim.

"Joe, I never—"

"I met you halfway by doing this, Jenny. I didn't have to go to the trouble."

She bowed her head, more than a tiny bit guilty that she had thought to manipulate Joe when he had obviously tried to do something so nice for her.

"However, I felt I had to do something when I saw how it upset you that the story couldn't keep generating as much attention as you thought it deserved. And knowing you, I understood that was about what was good for the town, not your ego." He shook his head, perhaps even clucked his tongue under his breath. "My question is, what are you willing to do to help this new campaign succeed?"

"What am I—" She went back over the conversation for a clue to when she had lost control. She knew she had been had, but she didn't quite know how it had happened or how to wriggle out of it, except to play innocent. "Do you want me to take those extra copies of the paper to other places?"

"No."

"No?"

"No." He unfolded his arms just a little, shifted his weight and said, "I want *us* to."

"Us?" The single syllable squeaked out of her tight throat.

"Before you get all worked up again, let me point out that you are the best ambassador both for Cupid's Corner and your pet project, right?"

She had to concede that, even though she knew in doing so she was leaving herself open to whatever diabolical plan Joe had up his rolled-back sleeve. "Yes, I suppose I am."

"And I am the one who has the contacts and who represents the paper and is able to negotiate on its behalf, right?"

"Yes, yes," she muttered, grudgingly going along with his reasoning.

"Then who better to take the publicity tabloid to outlying areas, especially ones with plenty of tourists and Route 66 connections, to spread the word about our events and bring in more people?"

"Okay. Okay, fine. I will grant you that." She sighed, feeling only a tiny bit defeated in her purpose of staying away from Joe entirely. "After all, there are only twelve miles of old Route 66 in Kansas. How long could it take?"

"Not long if we stayed in Kansas, but frankly, that territory has been covered by word of mouth, if nothing else. We'll make some stops here, of course. But the road trip I'm planning includes the stretch from Joplin, Missouri, to Miami, Oklahoma."

"Joplin to Miami? Oh no. No. That would take too long." Did he hear that panicky waver in her voice?

"Naw, we'd do it in day trips, coming back home every night." He dropped his arm over her shoulder as if he were amicably convincing an old fishing buddy to go try out a new lake. "It'd take two days, three tops, and it would be one terrific way to promo your project."

Two days, maybe three in the company of Joe. Did she dare do it?

The real question was, how could she not? What Joe did

not know, what she had chosen not to reveal to him, were her fears that her great once-in-a-lifetime promotion for the town would fall miserably short.

Of course now, she thought as she studied his glittering dark eyes, she was glad she had not told him about those reservations. How much more persuasive power would he have in this scenario if he knew that, though they had crossed over the halfway mark time-wise and gone a little over it wedding-wise, there were not enough weddings booked in advance right now to even tie the old record? They needed any and all publicity they could muster, and they needed it now. The success of the wed-a-thon and the new record were at stake here.

"So what do you say, Your Honor?"

"I say…" Jenny bit her lower lip. She looked at Joe with his heart-stopping grin. She thought of the promises she had made to her town and her duty to it and its residents to try everything to fulfill those promises, even at the cost of some personal inconveniences. She jerked her back straight, pushed his arm away from her shoulders, and held her head high. "I say…I say what choice do I have? I can't promise I can take three days away from my job, but I know I can take one and if I absolutely have to, two."

"Is that a yes?"

Jenny gave a sharp nod. "When do we leave?"

※　～

"Jennifer Fox, you are not seriously considering gallivanting around the countryside with…with…with him." Doc Dreamboat settled himself on the corner of Jenny's desk in the spacious but drab mayor's office and waved his hand in Joe's general direction.

"I don't think there will be any gallivanting involved, Doctor." Joe rounded the desk from the other side, his arms laced over his chest. When he stopped just a foot away from Jenny's swivel chair, he anchored his feet wide in a stance that hinted at possessiveness and immovability.

He had wormed his way into this meeting with the two of them here quite by accident, having run into the concerned doctor on the steps of City Hall after Joe had walked Jenny back to work. Still, that did not make Joe the least bit reserved about saying what was on his mind. He'd say whatever he felt compelled to say to keep the man who had once hurt Jenny from ever getting a chance to repeat the performance. "Fact is, Dr. Michaels, I don't even know what gallivanting is, but I do promise to try my best to avoid it whenever possible."

"Spare us the wisecracks, Avery. You know good and well what I mean, and if you don't—too bad. I wasn't talking to you anyway; I was addressing Jenny." He took Jenny's hand and began to pat it. "She's the one who's had a rough day. She's the one I came here to check on. If you had a shred of decency, you'd leave us alone so I can see for myself that she's all right."

"Oh, sure, it's her health you're worried about." Joe tried to snatch up her other hand in one of his but in his zeal missed and snagged her by the wrist, leaving her hand dangling from his grasp like a dead fish. "*That's* why you want to be alone with her. You're so concerned about her fragile state that the very first thing you did was attack her for doing her job. You never even asked how she is or why she even went to the clinic in the first place."

"*You* never gave me the chance." The hand patting became almost a light slapping.

Jenny scowled at her ex-fiancé, but he never seemed to notice her displeasure with him.

Joe sure wasn't going to be the one to point it out to the man. Let him annoy her all he wanted.

"No, not you. You never gave me a chance to talk to Jenny at all," the doctor accused. "That's not the way they do things where you're from, I suppose."

Joe felt Jenny flinch, but was it at Michaels's sneering tone or at the reminder that Joe was still an outsider in their small town? He wanted to say something equally caustic about the other man, to mention that while Michaels might be from Cupid's Corner, his plans included permanent residence in Kansas City. But even in the heat of anger, and especially to win a totally pointless argument, Joe could not reveal what he had been told in confidence. He clenched his teeth and let Alex keep talking.

"No, you just barged in here uninvited and started making noises about this big trip you think you're going to take with Jenny."

"If you'd been listening you'd have heard me say that Jenny and I are going to do a couple of day trips, nothing big, nothing outrageous."

"That you would try to whisk her off and have her all to yourself is outrageous enough, Avery."

"So we finally come to the truth of it. This isn't about Jenny's health, it's about me." Joe jabbed one finger into his breastbone. He would not normally have been so aggressive, but when it came to Jenny and her happiness, something primal in him came to the surface. Joe might not ever have her for himself, but he also would not stand by and let this man have her, only to discard her again when he realized he could not change her mind about leaving Cupid's Corner.

Joe took some small pride in knowing just then that he had succeeded in one area in which Alex Michaels had failed. He had her promise that she'd go away with him, even if it was only for a day at a time. Joe was getting Jenny out of town—no wonder it galled Michaels so.

Joe gave Jenny's wrist a swing, and her hand flicked up and down. Something in him registered that this unaccustomed passiveness from the feisty mayor was not a good sign, yet he could not simply stop everything now.

He locked gazes with the golden-haired doctor and pressed on. "Let's face it, Michaels, if Jenny had chosen to go off with Nurse Pritchet or Bobbie Ann or even kindly ol' Doc Hobbs, you wouldn't even be here now trying to keep her from going on this trip. For a man of medicine, you're awfully afraid of a little healthy competition."

Alex's fair complexion went beet red in the hollows of his cheeks. His lips worked as if forming some words better left unspoken in a lady's company, but he did not say anything. A spot of spittle frothed at the corner of his pale, taut lips. His eyes squeezed into threatening slits that did not hide his contempt for the object in his line of vision, namely Joe.

Joe stood his ground, his attitude caught between amused cockiness and sober protectiveness toward Jenny. "Admit it," he challenged the flushed-faced doctor glaring at him over Jenny's head. "I'm the reason you don't want her to go. I'm the one you have a problem with."

Alex looked toward the ceiling as if he might find some guidance in its peeling paint. When he lowered his gaze again, the heat had gone from his face, and it was Jenny, not Joe, he looked at and spoke to. "I have a problem, Jenny, with you getting so overwrought by all your responsibilities that it drove you to my clinic in the middle of the day."

"*I* drove Jenny to *the* clinic, and it was for her privacy's sake, not because she needed to see a doctor, least of all you."

"And now, to hear you want to take on more, when what you really should do is step back and relax?" Michaels shook his head in that way a doctor has of imposing guilt about a decision without really forbidding his patient to do something. "If you are going to go anywhere, it should be someplace that you can get your rest. For once, Avery had a good idea when he mentioned your sister. Why don't you let me take you up to Kansas City for the weekend to visit Bobbie Ann?"

And score some heavy-duty points for yourself, Joe thought. He gritted his teeth, knowing he could not say aloud what he was thinking without touching on the conversation he promised he would not share with anyone.

"Jenny, he's just trying to distract you from the things you really love and care about, your project and—"

"And *you?*" Michaels challenged.

"No, I never said she loved me." She loved him? Hearing it had a more jarring effect on Joe than he could have imagined. Jarring because he knew the words were false, and for once in his life, he wished they weren't. For once in his life, he wished a woman loved him, just a little bit—enough to give him the opportunity to find out if he loved her too.

"Jenny." Michaels cradled her delicate hand in his. "I won't pretend I like the idea of you going off alone with this...with him. I won't pretend it didn't hurt me to hear the rumors that flew after the incident on the Fourth of July—"

"I stumbled," Jenny blurted out.

At the exact same time, Joe tensed, pointed his finger at

the doctor, and growled out over Jenny's protest, "That was completely innocent, and it had nothing to do with you. *You* walked out on her, not the other way around. You haven't got any business coming back to town now and—"

"That's it! I've had it." Jenny stood with such force that her chair went wheeling drunkenly backward until it banged into the cream-colored wall. "Both of you, out of my office. Now!"

Both men stood there, eyes wide, blinking.

"I won't be fought over another minute by two men who seem more concerned with besting each other than with what's best for me." She flung her arm out, directing them toward the door. "Obviously, you two have feelings for me and whether I like it or not—and believe me, I do not like it—I have feelings for both of you too."

For the first time all summer, actually for the first time since he'd met Jenny Fox, Joe's heart lightened with hope about the potential of their relationship. She had feelings for her ex-fiancé *and* for Joe. Right now things appeared pretty equally weighted between the two men in Jenny's perception: She looked as though she wanted to strangle them both. So all Joe had to do was wait out the fine young doctor.

After all, in a month Michaels would go back to his search for the perfect home in Kansas City and an exciting position with an emergency room there. Joe, on the other hand, would still be here. If he did nothing else but wait, Joe would prove the winner yet in this showdown, as long as Jenny didn't pull any surprises on them. Joe felt sure she wouldn't. She'd acted so cautious all summer, why would she choose to do anything rash or even different now?

"I can't take this anymore. The petty bickering, the subterfuge, the constant battle on my part not to think about either of you. I can't take it. So I've just now decided I am going to have to take the proactive approach."

"What are you saying, Jenny?" Joe understood the term. He just wasn't sure how this woman with the soft hair, shining eyes, delicate skin, and resolve as hard as a rock intended to apply it.

"I'm saying that both of you have asked for some time alone with me, out of my element, as it were, to try to prove how good we'd be together." She sighed and shut her eyes. "You can call it much-needed rest or work for the end-of-the-summer events, but in the end we all know you're just jockeying for position, trying to come out ahead of each other in my affections. So I say, let's do it."

"What?" both men asked at once.

"Let's go on the trips—Alex, you can show me around Kansas City next weekend while I stay with Bobbie Ann and Mark."

Joe curled his hand into a fist at his side, then released it again in a moment of anxious energy.

"And Joe, we'll go on your publicity tour along old Route 66."

He grinned and noticed the slightest tinge of color rise in her cheeks.

"But let me warn you both." She raised her finger and tossed back the hair that fell across her rigid shoulder. "As hard as you'll be trying to show me that I belong with you, I'll be working to show you just how much it could never work. In the end, this may just be a case of 'Be careful what you wish for,' gentlemen—because you may just get it.

"I will not play games or try to sugarcoat anything about who I am, what I expect, and what I want from life. I will not pretend we can work out our differences later, but instead will strive to show you both just how truly insurmountable those differences can be. You may get some time alone with me—but by the time I'm through with you, that might be the last thing on earth you want."

"You have reached the home of Jennifer Fox, Mayor of Cupid's Corner, Kansas. I am currently unavailable to take your calls. If this concerns town business, a request for information on tourism, local events, or our record-breaking summer wed-a-thon, please call me again Monday morning at City Hall. If it is an emergency, you may contact City Hall now, and the operator will direct your call. If this is a personal call, please leave a message—unless you are someone simply trying to confirm the rumor that I have run off with Alex Michaels. In that case, let me say emphatically that I have gone to visit my sister and her husband, who live near but not in Kansas City, where Dr. Michaels is spending the weekend. If you still believe there is more to this story than that, I am sure you will find plenty of people willing to speculate on it with you at the café, in the fellowship hall after church, or around the mailbox on Main Street. I will not be making further comment on it, y'all, so don't bother calling me back to ask for more details. Thank you and have a nice day."

Beep.

—*message on Jenny Fox's answering machine for August 3–5*

Ten

August 4

"So, who caught the bridal bouquet?" Pritchy called from her kitchen's screen door just as Joe reached the first step that led to the apartment he rented from her, over the garage behind her house.

He stopped, turned, let what he was carrying slide to the ground, then shaded his eyes with his hand as he looked across the driveway. He could just barely make out her plump face with her nose all but smashed into the mesh of the screen door in one of the most blatant—and endearing—displays of nosiness Joe had ever experienced.

He put one foot on the bottom step and leaned back against the sun-warmed faded blue siding of the free-standing garage. "One of the bride's friends caught the bouquet. She had the fix in. It went right to the girl, and just before it got to her, she whipped out a catcher's mitt and made sure she didn't miss the throw."

Pritchy laughed. "Sounds fun. You got the pictures?"

"That's why I went, wasn't it?" He nudged the black camera bag on the ground beside him with his toe. "With Larry helping get the PR tabloid ready, somebody had to keep up with local news coverage—and what else did *I* have going on this weekend?"

"You mean besides pouting and moping and missing Jenny?" she asked, her face still framed by the scalloped edges of the screened window in the door.

He started to deny her assessment of his activities, but he didn't have the stomach to soft-pedal the truth. And Pritchy would not believe it anyway. The woman knew people; she knew their quirks and frustrations as well as what made them laugh and what kept them awake nights. She understood far more than most in town gave her credit for, far more than she let on. That's what made her such a good nurse for the small-town clinic and why Joe valued her opinion above that of almost any other person he'd met here.

"Well, what with all that picture taking and the moping and such, it seems to me you do have yourself a pretty full weekend," she called out to him over the black driveway, tweaking his conscience with a touch of motherly tenderness thrown in for good measure. "Don't suppose you'd have room in that kind of crowded schedule for supper with a tubby, gray-haired, widowed, professional-minded landlady, would you?"

"Are you kidding?" Joe rubbed his hands together in mock greedy glee. "Tubby, gray-haired, widowed, professional-minded landladies are my type of women! In fact, that's the kind of woman I am considering having supper with exclusively from this day forward."

"You should be so lucky," she teased. "But I have to warn you, we'll have a chaperon—Doc's coming over."

"Then just who will be chaperoning *who*, my fair landlady?" Joe wiggled his brows.

Pritchy giggled. She *giggled!*

Joe made a mental note of the reaction. Could it be that,

after all these years of working so closely together, romance had finally come to Doc Hobbs and his nurse?

"Now, don't go reading anything into Doc's stopping by," Pritchy suddenly warned as if she knew what Joe had just thought. "Every day for the last I-don't-know-how-long I have been telling that man what to do. I told him when to arrive at work and when to break for lunch. I was the one who locked up the doors and forced him to go home all those years after his wife had passed away and he would rather have stayed at the clinic 'round the clock to avoid going back to his empty house."

Joe smiled, though he knew Pritchy could not see his expression through the fine gray mesh and across the drive. He smiled because that's what the notion of Nurse Pritchet and Doc Hobbs inspired in him, a kind of warmth and happiness, a reassuring comfort about the basic goodness of life in general and in Cupid's Corner specifically. "You've been awfully good for Doc, Pritchy."

"Well, he's been plenty good to me too, Joseph. He let my kids come to the clinic to do their homework after school so that being a working mother, I didn't lose that crucial time with them." Pritchy's voice grew thin and far away, but Joe could still hear every word she said in loving admiration about her longtime employer. "When I lost my husband, he was always ready with a kind ear to listen to my grief. That was more than a decade ago, and since that time, with our children grown and moved away, Doc and I sort of became each other's family, I reckon."

"That's nice." As soon as he whispered his thoughts, Joe realized that Pritchy never could have heard him. Still, she seemed to respond to the bobbing of his head in agreement by giving him a nod in return.

Groaning a long, drawn-out sigh, she laughed at her own

reminiscences, then went on. "Doc and I depended on each other, that's for sure. Of course, he depended on me far more than I ever did on him. I swear, that man can't tie his own bow ties to save his life, and left to his own devices, he'd eat cottage cheese and bologna on white bread each and every meal of his life."

Joe winced, not because of Doc's diet but at the memory of the hot-dog-and-canned-peach fare he pretty much lived on, except for the days he arranged to be at the Wholly Mac-aroni Pasta Emporium for lunch at the same time Jenny ate there. He tugged at his own tie, which never did quite hang right, and swallowed hard.

"That why Doc's coming over tonight, really," Pritchy said.

"To have you tie his tie or to eat something besides cot-tage cheese and bologna?" Joe scratched his scalp as he tried to decipher what the woman was talking about.

"Well, I was going to say he was coming over because he always seeks me out when he needs someone to set him straight on anything. However, now that you mention it, Doc's been away from the clinic a goodly time. I daresay he might be primed for a good meal at that." Pritchy laughed. "To hear that old goat tell it, he's coming over because we got him one of those newfangled pagers to use while he's on call this weekend, covering while Dr. Michaels is off with…while he's away. Doc says he's afraid he isn't using it right because it hasn't gone off all weekend."

"Is it unusual for the weekends around here to be so quiet?" Joe asked, racking his brain for the last time the newspaper had run a story about any weekend emergency for the clinic.

"Heavens, no! There's not any good reason for Doc to even have that pager except that Dr. Michaels wanted to loan it to him, sort of showing off, if you ask me. The odds of us having to use it on any given weekend for the clinic are pretty small." Pritchy gave a snort. "In fact, the only reason Dr. Michaels got himself that pager was so his Realtor could get ahold of him while he's living out 'on the corner of nowhere,' as he calls the place where he grew up."

"So you know about his Realtor?"

"I said too much already. As the clinic nurse, it's not my place to gossip about the doctor or repeat anything he told me in private. Very unprofessional. Very unprofessional indeed."

"I know what you mean. He asked me to keep it off the record. So naturally, I haven't mentioned it to anyone, least of all Jenny." He pushed away from the building he'd been leaning on and sighed. "I hate holding back something like that from her, something that could eventually cause her so much pain."

"Or make her finally focus herself one way or another."

Joe squinted toward the house, noting that Pritchy had drawn back so that she seemed no more than a shadow in the door.

"Having Jenny focus on what's best for her once and for all, whether that is to let go of the past or to look for her future someplace else, is not the worst thing that could happen, Joe. Even if what she chooses doesn't suit your way of thinking, even if it hurts you a little now, it's so much better than what she has been doing."

"What she has been doing?"

"Maybe I should have said what she hasn't been doing." Pritchy laughed. "Not deciding, hiding from her feelings, coasting when she could be cruising, that's what's really bad for Jenny—and for you, too, believe me."

Joe took a step toward the door, then froze and shook his head. "I'm...I'm not sure what you're talking about, Pritchy."

"I'm talking about fishing or cutting bait. It's time Jenny decided if she's going to lament over getting hurt by one man for the rest of her life or if she's going to try to love again."

Love who? Joe wanted to demand, but he wasn't sure he really wanted to hear the answer to that question yet.

"Take it from a woman who has spent the last ten years alone, trying to convince herself that she didn't really need to ever love another man again. Someone who has been a little too comfortable with the way things are to even think about the way that things *could* be."

"You're talking about you and Doc now, aren't you?"

"When he called today with the ridiculous excuse about the pager, I realized just how much I had missed the old coot these last few weeks as he's played at retirement and I've gone on working." Laughter rang out from the woman in the kitchen. "I invited him to supper on the spot, and I've been walking around on air every time I think that I'm going to see him again this evening."

"Good for you." Joe gave her the thumbs-up. "Then I guess this means you really don't want me to come over for supper tonight?"

"On the contrary, Joseph. I need you here—to make sure things don't go all awkward or, worse yet, sour between Doc and me."

"And if they don't go all awkward and sour between you and Doc?"

"Well, I invited you for supper." Her voice took on an almost lyrical quality. "That does not necessarily mean you have to hang around for dessert!"

"Yes ma'am." He gave her a curt salute, then turned on his heel to go upstairs to his bleak apartment.

"Be here around six!" Pritchy's voice carried after him.

Joe waved at her over his shoulder to let her know he

understood. He stopped long enough to sling his camera bag over his shoulder, then started his weary climb. As he trudged up the creaking staircase, thick with white paint that looked as if it might have been mixed with some of Doc's favored cottage cheese, he mulled over everything he'd just learned.

He had never stopped to realize the full import of a relationship that had gone on as long as Doc and Pritchy's. He marveled that it had endured so much and yet still had the capacity to change and grow. How he wished he saw a relationship like that in his future.

Though he could well envision Jenny and himself in their present adversarial roles well into their twilight years, he wondered what else might lie in store. He did know that what was going on in Kansas City right now might spell the end for anything more to ever blossom between them.

❧   ❧

"What are you doing back so early?" Bobbie Ann sat forward on the big green sofa in her family room. Jenny could see the outline of her craning her neck to call out as Jenny strolled through the front door. "Did Alex's friend's party break up so soon?"

"Oh no, the party is still going strong. So is Alex." Jenny hung her purse on the coatrack in the hallway, rolled her neck slowly to release some of the tension built up in those muscles, then started toward the back of the house where her sister, no doubt, wanted to hear all the details of her evening.

The clock on the mantel struck ten o'clock just as Jenny slumped into the seat next to Bobbie Ann.

"What's wrong, honey? Were Alex's doctor friends rude to you?"

Jenny smiled at the sisterly concern on Bobbie Ann's face. "What are you going to do if they were? Go knock them down and tell them to be nice to your baby sister or else?"

"I was eight when I did that to Larry Hackerman, Jenny." Bobbie Ann hugged a throw pillow to her chest and rocked back against the sofa cushions. "You'd think you'd have forgotten about it by now."

"Well, I haven't." She gave her sister's arm an affectionate pinch. "And apparently neither has Larry. You know he never has let them run an unflattering picture of me in the paper? I think I have your little…talk with him all those years ago to thank for that."

"He's never run an unflattering picture of you because you couldn't take an unflattering picture if you tried." Bobbie Ann flicked at one stiffly sprayed curl tumbling from Jenny's perfectly arranged topknot. "So there."

Jenny's thoughts flew back to the first day she'd realized Alex was in town. When Alex had gotten stuck in the chair and she'd reacted so badly and everyone had been in such an uproar. She had to laugh at herself, while at the same time feeling hugely grateful to Larry—and if she was being brutally honest, to his editor, Joe—for not running what must have been a classically comical photo. "If you only knew just how truly horrific a picture I can take, Bobbie Ann. If you only knew."

She must have looked awful at the moment Larry flashed his camera at them, Jenny thought. Anxious and agitated, totally caught off guard and wishing she were anywhere else in the world—about the way she had felt at the party tonight.

"So, that doesn't explain why you're home so early,

kiddo. If I promise not to storm over and crash the party and start bullying the guests, will you tell me what happened?" Bobbie Ann drew her legs under her and depressed a button on the TV remote to mute the news program she'd been watching. "Were they rude to you? Where's Alex? Why didn't you invite him in?"

Jenny chuckled, reached up, and unfastened the clip holding her hair up, then shook her head, relishing the feel of relief from her scalp to her toes. "To answer your questions in opposite order, I didn't invite Alex in because he didn't bring me home."

"He didn't?"

"It was out of his way and he wasn't ready to go." Jenny held no animosity toward the man for that, and she hoped to make sure Bobbie Ann wouldn't either. "I caught a ride with someone who works at a hospital near here and had to report in for the eleven-o'clock shift."

"With a stranger?"

"A doctor, a friend of Alex's."

"That doesn't sound like—"

"Actually, Bobbie Ann, that ride might prove one of the best things about this weekend. It gave me some insight and ideas about getting another doctor for the clinic. As for Alex, don't forget he hadn't seen any of his friends since he came back to Cupid's Corner. So I insisted he stay at the party."

"Okay, that explains Alex's whereabouts, but what about my other question? Did you want to leave early because they didn't make you feel comfortable at the party?"

"Nothing like that." Jenny shook her head. "Nobody was mean or rude to me. Quite the opposite, in fact. Once they discovered my official capacity as mayor they were duly impressed and respectful. They sought me out to ask me questions and compliment me on doing my civic duty, you know, that kind of thing. And when I told them a little bit about the wed-a-thon—"

"Goodness, you told them about *that*?"

"People asked." Jenny shrugged, then let a devious grin appear on her lips. "You think I'm going to pass up a promotional opportunity like that? To get the word out to a bunch of doctors and their significant others about our quaint little community? The place where they might want to visit and spend their cold hard cash?"

"So you told them."

"I told them." Jenny gave one firm nod, which sent the coils of her hair bouncing over her cheeks and neck. "What's more, several of them said they'd like to come down and see us and that if they knew anyone looking to elope, they'd make sure they knew about our town."

"Well, good for you then."

"Good for Cupid's Corner," she corrected her sister.

"Interesting though."

"What's that?"

"Well, you'd think that, being friends of Alex's, they'd have heard of the place before."

"You'd think, wouldn't you?" Jenny folded her arms and realized her lips were pressed tightly to her teeth.

"Okay, let's hear it. What's the real reason you left so early? Did you and Alex have a fight?"

"How can you have a fight with someone if that person is totally ignoring you?"

"Were you ignoring Alex or the other way around?" Bobbie Ann cocked her head and snuggled down into the comfy sofa like a person settling in for a really good story.

"He ignored me—well, not *ignored* really. More like, stuck me out for display then forgot about me." Jenny sat down, slipped off her simple black pumps, pulled up the legs of her dressy black pants, and kicked her feet up into her sister's lap. "Honestly, Bobbie Ann, he made me feel like a trophy."

"Hey, why not? You are a prize catch." Bobbie Ann mugged and winked, then grew quietly serious. "Think about it, sweetie, he lost you once. Can you blame him if he feels a little proud to have you on his arm again?"

"That's the problem, Bobbie Ann. I wasn't anywhere near his arm."

"And you wish you had been? On his arm? *In* his arms?" Bobbie Ann giggled, resting her chin on the pillow she was holding.

Jenny gazed at her sister, her heart filled with memories. In her soft cotton nightgown and with her hair pulled into a braid, Bobbie Ann looked like the girl Jenny had shared her secrets with all through their childhood. They'd talked of everything in those days, shared every thought, hope, and dream. Back then, though, their greatest troubles seemed nothing more than what they wanted to do when they grew up and which boy would sit by them in Sunday school—and whether or not that meant he would be their true love.

Bobbie Ann had found her true love, and Jenny had fulfilled her wildest dreams about what she wanted to be when she grew up. They had both aimed for what mattered most to each of them and still had so many hopes left to look forward to, Jenny thought. To be anything but completely honest with her sister at this point in their lives was unthinkable to Jenny.

"Oh, Bobbie Ann, he…he lied to me. Just like when we were engaged." Jenny took her sister's hand and gave it a squeeze. That helped her hold back the tears that bathed her eyes and threatened to spill onto her cheeks, but it did little to keep her feelings back. "He let me believe that there was some chance that he might stay in Cupid's Corner, knowing full well that as long as that was a possibility, I could never move on and really, truly get over him. How could he do that to me? How could I fall for that same shabby treatment twice?"

"Oh, honey. What happened? How do you know all this?"

"I overheard him at the party. He told one of his friends that he had several homes lined up to look at tomorrow." The humiliation she had felt at the party welled up again. How could she have been so naive? So trusting? Hadn't she learned her lesson before? She sniffled and looked up, trying not to let her pain and embarrassment at her lapse of judgment break through in her voice. "He kept going on about how he would never consider living anywhere but this neighborhood or that one, all of them in Kansas City, of course."

"Oh, Jenny, I…" Bobbie Ann simply leaned in and wrapped her into a big hug. "You really wanted this to work out with Alex this time, didn't you?"

"Oh my, no!" Jenny pulled away. "No, I really *didn't*. What I did was let that man make a first-class idiot out of me all over again, and I didn't even want to pursue a real relationship with him!"

"You didn't? Then why'd you say all that stuff on the Fourth of July about realizing you hurt him and hinting that you might give him a second chance?"

"I just wanted to know that there wasn't anything left between us, that's all. That I wouldn't have any regrets. I wanted a clean break this time, if there was going to be a break." She looked around, spotted a box of tissues, and grabbed up two or three as she went on talking. "Most of all I wanted to finally mend that hole he left in my confidence when he lied to me and thought it wouldn't change our relationship. Big joke on me, huh?"

"The only joke in this mess is Alex. And calling him a big joke is definitely too kind, if you ask me."

"The worst of it is, I knew deep down that I didn't want to start anything serious with Alex again." Jenny dabbed at her eyes. "That's how pathetic I am when it comes to dealing with the opposite sex. Even men I don't like can tromp on my feelings and play me for a fool." She blew her nose loudly, then chuckled along with her tears of self-pity. "Maybe I should just get a cocker spaniel."

Bobbie Ann laughed. "Maybe you should just get in touch with what you really want."

Jenny jerked her chin up, determined to put aside her unproductive emotions and move on. "What I really want is to forget about men and romance entirely and just focus on being the best mayor my town ever had."

"No, you don't." Bobbie Ann shook her head and laughed just a little.

"Oh, like *you* know what I want."

"I should. I've listened to you talk about it enough in all our sisterly chats. I've watched you, how you handle yourself, the things you cherish, the things that make you laugh and cry. I know you, little sister. I know you want a full life, a godly home, healthy children, work with a purpose, good friends, the fellowship of church and family, and romance."

"No." Jenny gave a sad but firm shake of her head. "Not romance."

"Yes, romance! With a decent guy who won't lie to you or take you or your feelings for granted. A man who wants the same things you want but knows, like you would if you'd ever let it through that thick skull of yours, that those things may take risk and sometimes compromise."

Jenny wadded the tissues up in her lap and said nothing. Her sister made a lot of sense. While her mind was able to grasp it, her heart was still too tender to even let her talk about it anymore.

"What you want, little sister, is a man who is a true friend, shares your faith and family ideals, and when you look deep into his eyes"—she raised both hands, then opened them, fingers spread wide, in one explosive movement—"skyrockets!"

"Please! I've had enough skyrockets in my summer already." Jenny jumped on the chance to lighten the moment, to get the talk away from all things romantic and onto something that seemed more suited to her real life lately—embarrassing herself in public. "Do you know how long it has taken for people to finally stop teasing me about that incident on the Fourth? Believe me, after that fiasco, if there's one thing I don't want more of, it's skyrockets."

"Fine, we won't talk skyrockets," Bobbie Ann eagerly agreed. "Which brings us right to the topic of Joe Avery, doesn't it?"

"Joe Avery is not a topic, Bobbie Ann." Jenny felt her face go hot, her skin prickle at the very notion that the stubborn, arrogant editor was anything more to her than a passing curiosity. "He's a…a…footnote in the long, complicated, and sometimes twisted narrative of my life."

"Just a footnote, huh?" Bobbie Ann shook her head as she let her tone underscore her doubt.

"If that much." Jenny waved the thought away. "He means nothing to me. Really. How can he? He's only a temporary blot on the timeline of our town, while I am determined to become a permanent fixture there."

"And if he weren't temporary?"

Jenny, not wasting any of her brilliant debating skills on this argument, simply growled, "He is."

"But if he weren't?"

"I said 'he is,' Bobbie Ann, so what's the use in speculating otherwise?" Jenny snapped. "He's blown into town on a lark, or at the very least as a step to build his résumé, to tack on the title 'Editor' before he applies for a better job in a bigger city."

Bobbie Ann leaned in, a mixture of shock and disbelief on her face. "He told you this?"

"No," Jenny admitted, unhappy at having to do so. She would not look her sister in the eye as she went on. "He told me just the opposite. He says he wants to stay in town, but I'm no fool. He knows what kind of girl I am, what kind of commitments I have, what kind of things I find admirable in others, and he's just showing me what I want to see."

"Oh, Jenny." Bobbie Ann put her hand on Jenny's arm. "I had no idea that Alex had hurt you this badly—that you wouldn't be able to trust anyone else because of his actions."

"I'm not acting hurt, Bobbie Ann." Jenny jerked her arm away. She lowered her feet from Bobbie Ann's lap and sat, ramrod straight on the couch, her chin up and her hands in her lap. "I'm just being smart. Knowing what I know about how smothering small-town life can be for someone who doesn't want to live that way with all their heart. Then seeing how talented, ambitious, and capable Joe is, I just know he will eventually leave Cupid's Corner. For that reason I will never let myself care anything about him."

"Oh, honey." Bobbie Ann's voice took on the kind but unwavering quality of their mother's. "Don't you think it's a little too late for that?"

"What do you mean?" Jenny refused to admit she even suspected what her sister had in mind.

"Listen to yourself, how you describe him. Your eyes light up when you talk about him. Don't you see how just mentioning his name brings out such volatile emotions in you, girl?" Bobbie Ann put her arm over Jenny's shoulders and gave a light but firm squeeze. "For someone who is just a *foot*note in your life, Joe Avery certainly seems to have gone completely to your head."

HOWDY, FRIEND
YOU'RE ENTERING
BAXTER SPRINGS
FIRST COW TOWN IN KANSAS

Founded 1858
Chamber of Commerce

—*real sign at the city limits of
Baxter Springs, Kansas*

Eleven

"Did I ever tell you that when I decided I would leave my job in St. Louis and move to a small town in Kansas, I was thinking of Baxter Springs?" Joe slowed his car as this stretch of Route 66 turned into the business district of the neighboring town on a street now called Military Avenue.

In truth, Baxter Springs's business district was no busier than downtown Cupid's Corner; both had suffered the ravages of time and neglect, partly due to the fact that bypasses had long ago diverted most of the traffic along easier, faster routes. She looked out the dusty windshield at the stretch of small town, to the brick building that still bore the faded word *Undertaker* painted on its side, even as Joe pulled up to one of the landmarks of the Mother Road, Murphey's Restaurant. She tried to imagine Joe as a citizen of this town instead of her own, but she couldn't—not because Joe seemed so tied to her sleepy little smidge-on-the-map town, but because he did not seem to fit here as a permanent fixture any more than he fit in Cupid's Corner.

Jenny had given a lot of thought to that very fact since her long talk with Bobbie Ann and the uneventful weekend away with Alex. No matter what she did, she couldn't shake the idea that a talented go-getter like Joe could only go get himself somewhere else, somewhere better with more opportunity, more action, more everything. If, as Bobbie Ann had suggested, Joe had really gone to Jenny's head, then she was determined to make sure he did not take her heart with him when he left. That meant keeping her wits about her and her defenses always up.

She wouldn't even have come with him on this wild promotional trip if she didn't see how much it could benefit her town and its cause. Today they would shake hands and leave the *Arrow's* tourist advertising tabloid in Baxter Springs and Miami, Oklahoma; tomorrow they'd head out from Cupid's Corner east to Galena, Kansas, then on to Joplin, Missouri. After that she wouldn't spend any more time alone with Joe Avery than absolutely necessary.

"Jenny?"

She twisted sideways in the seat to face him, holding herself rigid and uninterested. "What?"

"I asked if I'd ever told you that when I decided to move to Kansas, I thought I would be coming to Baxter Springs?" He draped his wrist over the steering wheel. "I know it's not one of my usual riveting stories about my fascinating, thrill-a-minute life, but I didn't realize it could actually bore you into a coma—or is that some kind of hunger-induced trance?"

"Neither, I—" She cut herself off before she accidentally told him too much about her inner musings and the conclusions they'd led her to. "You said you thought you were coming to Baxter Springs? You mean there were two job openings and you thought you'd accept this one instead of taking over the *Arrow*?"

"No, no. Nothing like that." Joe laughed that deep, I-know-something-you-don't-know laugh that sent a wonderful shiver of familiarity and anticipation down Jenny's spine.

"I mean that when I was a little kid my folks used to drive from my hometown of Sapulpa, Oklahoma, through Kansas to visit my grandmother in Missouri. We took old Route 66 to avoid the toll road and because it took us through some great stuff, and I always remember stopping for a break in Baxter Springs. So when I got word that a small town on Route 66 was looking for an editor, I jumped at the interview, thinking it had to be Baxter Springs."

"Wait a minute. Wait just one childhood-memory-picking minute." Jenny pressed her fingertips to her temples, as if that might keep all the information she'd just taken in from slipping away before she could sort through it all. "I'll bypass for a moment the fact that you're telling me you came to roost in my beloved hometown by accident just so I can make sure I've got this straight. Are you saying you're from Oklahoma?"

He shifted in his seat, making the small car jiggle just enough to annoy her and make her aware of how close they sat in his cozy front seat.

"I was born in Tulsa, then my family moved to Sapulpa when I was two. My dad worked in the oil patch, so we went where the work was, all over Oklahoma and then Texas, usually in really small towns, you know the kind."

She nodded. Who knew small towns better than she did?

"Then came the oil bust. Jobs and money pretty much dried up. My family moved east, and that's where I got most of my education."

"And at least some of your attitude," she muttered through a teasing expression.

"Is that a smile I see on your face, Your Honor?" He peered closely at her. "Because if you are calling me what I think you are calling me—a Yankee—you had better be wearing a smile."

"I'm not calling you anything." She batted her lashes and held up her hands in a show of overplayed innocence. "I'm just saying—hey, why Baxter Springs?"

"Smooth way to change the subject, Mayor." He shook his head, and sunlight glinting off the shop windows created a curious halo effect against the blackness of his thick hair. "No wonder you're a whiz in politics."

"Oh no, you can't get out of this so easily. You said your family stopped in Baxter Springs. You implied that when you heard about a town on Route 66 with a job opening, you naturally assumed it was here and not Cupid's Corner?"

"Because my brother and I would never let my dad stop in Cupid's Corner."

"Oh?"

"Too mushy." He winced. "All the names of the stores—"

"Oh, so your problem with the names started way back before you even moved to our town?" She still couldn't fully grasp the idea of Joe having spent his early years in this part of the country, and her mind struggled to make the pieces fit.

"Not to mention the Cupid on the courthouse lawn; that's hardly the stuff of a little boy's dreams."

What about a big boy's dreams? she wanted to ask. *Did they include a town with silly-named businesses and Cupid on the courthouse lawn?* She bit her lower lip to keep from asking the prying question. Besides, she felt she knew the answer.

Why didn't he just come out and say it? Jenny tapped the toes of her simple canvas shoes on the protective gray plastic mat on the floorboard. Cupid's Corner had not been Joe's first choice as a place to live, and it would not be his last stop before settling down.

"Now Baxter Springs, see, it had a far more appealing history, from a boy's point of view, you understand." He lowered his head and swept his gaze across the panoramic view of the tiny town.

Jenny followed suit, trying to read more into the old familiar structures than she ever had before, trying to see them through the eyes of the exuberant young Joe. "How so? It looks to me pretty much like any other town you'd find around here."

"Well, you'd have to look beneath the surface, but it's there." He narrowed his eyes and pointed one finger at the restaurant where they had arranged to leave some promotional material. "Do you realize that this very building right here, Murphey's Restaurant, used to be a bank?"

She folded her arms. She was well aware of the many tales that circulated around the small towns in this corner of the state. She also had a pretty good idea which ones were fact and which were fantasy. "Yes, I've heard the story about the old bank."

"That Jesse James and Cole Younger once robbed it, then hightailed it out for Indian Territory?" He had the air of a kid spinning a wild adventure, and there was a light in his face that Jenny could see on a much younger version of the man. "And how they outwitted the posse sent after them and got away without firing a single shot?"

"You know many local historians don't hold with that story," she said softly, as if breaking bad news.

"But some do, and so do some folks around here." He raised an eyebrow.

She raised her eyebrow right back at him. "*Some* folks say this place is haunted by the ghosts of cowboys past too. But I don't believe that either." "Aw, you're just jealous because I found Baxter Springs more interesting as a kid than your so-called Hitchin' City." But he said it with a wink.

"Why should I be jealous of your misguided youth?" she

answered in kind, hoping he did not sense the undercurrent of her emotions for him and about the future she expected for him, in her reply.

"Misguided youth." He laughed. "C'mon, Jenny, even you have to admit that the history of this town, either real or imagined, would have had infinitely more appeal for my brother and me than the elopement capital of Route 66. What with the cow-town symbolism and all. Add to that the fact that Mickey Mantle played ball here for three years with the Baxter Springs Whiz Kids before moving on to a slightly more famous team, the New York Yankees."

She set her jaw firm, her gaze straight ahead. Without so much as a glance, she reached to her side to pluck up her favorite hat, the one Joe had mended. A shake of her hair to fan it away from her face and an upward tilt of her chin projected her no-nonsense mood perfectly, she decided as she fitted the hat down on her head. "Well, I guess anybody who really wants to make it big would have to move on, to get out of a small town to really and truly make something of themselves."

"I'm not sure where that remark came from, or if you intend it to impart some hidden message to me or to convey some feeling about me, Jenny, but I do know this."

He paused, in a way that commanded her full attention before he would go on.

Jenny felt the heat of his eyes on her profile.

He leaned toward her, the intensity of his concentration almost palpable.

She did not want to look at him but instinctively knew he would not finish his sentence until she met his steady gaze.

He remained absolutely silent.

Jenny gritted her teeth. She couldn't stand it. She *had* made the remark for all the reasons Joe had assumed, to impart the hidden message and convey her feelings about what she felt sure the future held in store for him. She couldn't stand not knowing his response. It might hurt to hear it straight from his lips, but then she'd know. She'd know that her fears regarding Joe's temporary status as a citizen of Cupid's Corner were well founded. That could only help her deal with her feelings, she reasoned.

"Oh, all right. You don't know where my remark came from, yadda-yadda-yadda, but you *do* know what, Joe?" She thrashed in her seat as she turned toward him, anxiety fueling her movements. "*What* is it you want to tell me that you know?"

"I know you're afraid to get involved with me because you think I'll pull a Jesse James or a Mickey Mantle or, more precisely, an Alex Michaels and hightail it out of town for a better opportunity." He took a deep breath.

Jenny involuntarily took one too.

Then he cleared his throat and hemmed and stammered for a moment before saying, "Of course, Doc Michaels is back now. Didn't want to imply that I knew anything different than that he's back to stay. That is, I—"

"He's not staying." Jenny touched her hair, coiling one dark strand around her finger. "He never had any intentions of moving back to stay. I think everybody pretty much takes that as a given, Joe. In fact, the whole time he's been living in Cupid's Corner, he's had a Realtor looking for a home for him to buy in Kansas City."

"So he said," Joe muttered.

"What?" Jenny heard him; she just wasn't sure how to interpret what she had heard.

"So—" Joe drew out the lone syllable, cleared his throat, then charged on. "So he said that to you then? That he has a Realtor looking for a place in the city for him?"

"I overheard him at a party. The next day I made some excuses about not feeling up to going out with him, and he pushed me to tell him why. Only after I confronted him with the truth did he come clean about it."

"Oh, you poor kid, finding out like that." He reached toward her.

She shrank away from his comforting touch, her mind and emotions swirling at the idea that not only had Alex kept his plans a secret from her, but Joe had as well. She wanted to sound aloof, detached, but when she opened her mouth she could only speak in a soft, hoarse whisper. "Yes, wouldn't it have been so much easier on me, so much less hurtful and humiliating if the news had come directly from someone I trusted?"

"Like Alex?"

"Like Alex—that would have been best, sure. But I was thinking of you, Joe." Disappointment filled her voice with hushed anguish. "How long have *you* known? And why didn't you say anything to me?"

He raked his fingers through his hair, glanced around, then made a grab for the button that lowered the windows. Over the electronic whir, he coughed and sputtered. "Is it hot in here? I think it's pretty hot in here."

"That long, huh?" she asked calmly.

He let out an almost noiseless chuckle, then looked her way. "Since the very first day he arrived in town. He asked me not to tell anyone, and so I honored his request."

"Even knowing how it could hurt me?"

"Yes. It wasn't easy, Jenny, but it was the right thing to do. I gave my word." He met her eyes with an unerring gaze that did not ask her to forgive him but seemed to hope she would understand why he had done it. "I didn't see this as keeping anything from you but as keeping my promise, both professionally and personally. I'm not in a line of work that's likely to make me rich or famous, or even all that respected by people in general. Being a man of honor, worthy of trust even by the person I see as my competition for the one thing I want most in life—that's all I have. Without it I'm nothing, Jenny."

"You know what, Joe?"

"What, Jenny?"

"You're a very decent guy." She said it with a touch of sadness and regret in her voice. That was just her way of letting him know that this did not really change anything between them. She still couldn't let herself give in to her emotions, knowing their relationship was probably ill-fated from the start. "Too bad things are…the way they are."

"Jenny." He reached out and took her hand, cradling it in the warmth of both of his. "I can't promise you that I will grow old and die in Cupid's Corner."

There. He'd said it. Just as she'd always suspected. What a shame that being right about this didn't make her feel one bit better about the news.

"I also can't promise that I won't do just that. I like Cupid's Corner, corny names and mushy history notwithstanding." He grinned.

She couldn't help but do the same, though her smile did not feel as broad and open as the one he gave her.

"I'd like to think that in your little town I've found a home, and in its people I've found true friends." He gave her hand a squeeze.

She dropped her gaze.

He lifted her chin with one finger, ducking his own head to make sure their eyes would meet as he went on. "I have no plans now to ever leave that place, those friends, my job, or…"

You. He did not say it, but it rang through the closed quarters just the same, as clearly as if he had spoken the single telling word in his deep, masculine voice.

Jenny's heart leapt. Her stomach clenched. She fought back the threat of impending tears with a sniffle and a flutter of her lashes.

"But I'm also not prepared to say that I will never go anywhere else, move anywhere else for as long as I live."

"I know," she murmured.

"No, you assumed. From the minute you met me, you assumed I'd be leaving town any day. That's how you've treated me, not like a member of the community but like an outsider. All because you don't think I'm going to stay put for the rest of my life." His dark eyes flashed, and the hollows of his lean cheeks reddened. His lips tightened against his white teeth, in a show of his frustration with her and her obvious attitude. "I'm not even thirty years old, Jenny. The idea that I would commit to that kind of closed-minded thinking about a town, no matter how charming I found it, is just not who I am."

"Are you saying I'm closed-minded because I never want to live anywhere else?" How had he turned this into something about her? "Hey, I wasn't the one who moved into your town, after all, and began asking you out. I didn't seek you out or pursue you. Just the opposite. I was just minding my own business, building the life I wanted. If you had never showed up, my life would be right on track, just like it is now, and for that you think you can just up and call me close-minded?"

"Yes." He released her hand and crossed his arms over his rumpled work shirt, dragging his already loosened tie down another half-inch. "I'm saying you're closed-minded because you won't even let yourself imagine the possibility that you might, someday, want to live anywhere else but Cupid's Corner. You won't even entertain the idea that you might find happiness or prosperity or even romance some-place else. Not that you have to go elsewhere to find those things, but that you *could*."

Jenny opened her mouth to protest, but she couldn't get anything to come out, so Joe rushed on with his keen and uncompromising observations.

"You're closed-minded, Jenny, because you choose to be that way, especially toward anyone who you don't think shares that same single-minded allegiance to Cupid's Corner as you do."

"Single-minded allegiance? That's kind of harsh, isn't it?"

"How would you describe your devotion to your town? A devotion that has cost you a wedding, a social life, even the prospect of watching your nephew grow up or living near your parents as they grow older, or creating a new home somewhere else with, oh, say a dashing newspaper-editor type?"

When he put it that way, weighing her steadfast loyalty to her town against all those things, her mind-set did seem a bit silly and shortsighted. That realization at once took her breath away, like a sucker punch to the stomach, and made her lightheaded with a kind of relief she hadn't known in a very long time. Still, the old defensiveness reared its head, and she felt obliged to remind him, "I have a great deal of responsibility in my town, Joe. People count on me, and they know I'll be there for them."

"This town existed a long time before you came along, Your Honor. And I have the feeling it won't crumble to dust the day you conclude your stint in office. Besides, would you listen to yourself a minute? Responsibilities? People count-ing on you? Hanging tough in a place because you think it can't withstand your absence is not the same as making a home someplace because it's where you want to be, with the people who matter most to you."

He had a point. She wished she could tell him he didn't, but she'd have to lie to do so. She found herself wondering, When had it happened that she stopped loving her town and let herself become trapped in it? Though she did not feel trapped exactly, Joe's description of her determination that she could never leave did make it sound that way.

"And it's too bad you feel this way, Jenny." His broad shoulders slumped in quiet defeat. "Because you're missing out on a lot of wonderful stuff. On dreaming about all the possibilities you can imagine for the future *as well as* building for the probabilities you can foresee. You're missing out on all the fun we could have had together, all the plans we could have laid and the memories we could have—" He cut himself off with a derisive snort. "What's the use even talking to you about it?"

"No, don't feel that way, Joe." She shut her eyes and chewed at her lip before getting up the nerve to go on. "For the first time since you got here, we've had the chance to talk, to really talk. I've learned about your personal history and gotten some real insight into…things. I…I'd hate to think you'd keep yourself from talking to me about this based on my own bad behavior these last few weeks."

"Months," he corrected with a hint of a smile.

"Years, if we're going to be perfectly honest." She laughed at herself and the all-too-real admission.

"Sorry if I sounded kind of angry and hurt, Jenny, but that's how I feel." He looked away, then fixed his attention fully on her, deep but undefined emotion and quiet sorrow shining in his eyes. "It's like I've tried everything I could just to connect with you, to try to let you know how much I admire and am attracted to you. Yet nothing I did has ever been enough. Unless I can promise you the one thing you'll never believe of me anyway—that I'll stay in town with you forever—you won't even give me a chance."

She wanted to deny that, but how could she deny the stark, unvarnished truth?

"I can make that kind of commitment to my God, my family, my friends, to always stay faithful, to never forsake them. I honestly think I could make that kind of commitment to a woman like you, Jenny." He searched her eyes with his unwavering gaze. "But I can't make that kind of pledge to a *place*. Frankly, I think it's a shame that you would demand it of anyone before you'd even try to get to know and care about them."

"But, Joe, I never meant it that way. I avoided getting involved with you because that seemed the wisest thing— the best way not to get hurt again."

"If you go through life trying not to get hurt, Jenny, it's a pretty good bet you're also not going to get loved."

"I don't want to miss out on being loved, Joe, or on loving…someone," she whispered.

He nodded. "You know, it's recently been brought to my attention that time's awastin', that life goes by too quickly and if you aren't careful you can lose the things you really count dear to you—or you can reach out now and grab on to them and hold on for all you're worth. But that takes a decision on your part, Jenny. You have to decide to take the risk."

They sat there in silence for a moment.

Jenny wished she knew the perfect thing to say to that, but she just wasn't sure. Sitting in a car in front of an old diner on Military Avenue in Baxter Springs was not the sort of place a girl like her usually made life-changing decisions.

Adding to her confusion and upset over the whole thing was the realization that she had entered this conversation hoping to force Joe to admit he wasn't going to settle down permanently in Cupid's Corner. She had not gotten that wish. He only admitted he thought about leaving, while acknowledging that he actually planned to stay put. And now, for the first time in years, Jenny found herself open to the idea that perhaps—just perhaps—she might one day be persuaded to leave her precious hometown herself.

"Well, are you ready?" Joe's voice intruded on her thoughts.

"Are you kidding?" she snapped. "I can't make up my mind about something this big this quickly. I have to—"

"Are you ready to go deliver the promo tabloids to the restaurant?" Joe opened the car door and gestured with a stack of papers over his arm toward Murphey's.

"Oh, ready to…to deliver…" Jenny blinked at the scene of the old building in the bright summer light. "Um, yes. Yes, *that* I am ready to do."

She popped open her car door and slid outside, glad for the diversion from the more serious issues she knew she must now address. Later, when she was alone, she would consider everything Joe had said. She didn't know how or whether it would change anything, but she fully understood that the things they'd talked about today *could* change everything, from her relationship with Joe to how—and maybe *where*—she lived the rest of her life.

Emergency Meeting
Town Council
Cupid's Corner, Kansas
Agenda

Old Business:
- Permits for Labor Day parade
- Parking for Labor Day festivities
- Status of wed-a-thon goals
- Status of final record-breaking weddings
- Budget request for Labor Day barbecue

New Business:
- Report on possible new doctor to run town clinic

—posted agenda for last-minute
town council meeting

Twelve

I want to thank you all again for coming to City Hall on such short notice, and on Friday evening, to boot."

Jenny stood in the doorway to the meeting room to express her gratitude to each and every member of the council who had turned out tonight. "If you hurry you may still be able to join the well-wishers for the fifty-eighth wedding this summer, so we've now passed the record set the year the town earned the title Hitchin' City, USA. The couple are in the chapel right about now, so if you want to wander over that direction, you'll probably make it there in time to toss some rice and cheer them as they leave. Maybe you can even prod a few single ladies into vying to see who can catch the bouquet."

"You gonna get yourself in line for that, Mayor?" a well-meaning woman asked, poking Jenny in the ribs with her elbow.

"Sorry, not in the job description," Jenny shot back with a smile just broad enough to stretch her credibility.

"You do recall how back in the beginning of all this hoo-ha the council recommended that if we fell shy of enough weddings, we might call upon you to step up to the plate, or the altar as the case may be," another citizen quipped as he shuffled past Jenny and out into the hallway.

"Lucky for me that thanks to contacts made in Kansas City and through the paper's publicity tabloid, we now have exactly enough weddings scheduled to make the count." Jenny laughed, but it was a weak laugh. She knew, after all, that one case of cold feet, one last-minute change of plans, one bride who opted out of elopement for fancier fare, and they could come up short of their goal. But while it was a nagging worry, nothing could spoil the moment: She had found a new doctor for the clinic, and the council had basically told her to do what was necessary to interview the candidate and finalize the arrangements.

The members mumbled good-byes and gave thumbs-up as they left the short but eventful gathering. One by one, Jenny shook each hand vigorously, patted backs, and even gave a couple of side-to-side hugs to the departing council members to make sure everyone felt the full scope of her appreciation for what they had accomplished in the nearly impromptu session.

At the rear of the meeting room, a lone figure hung back, looking more shadowy than usual in the twilight dimness. Still, she did not have to see Joe's face to know he was watching her. They'd hardly spoken since their long talk ten days earlier. Life, in the form of a doctor Jenny had met at the party with Alex, had intervened. The potential hiring of that doctor, her regular duties as mayor, and the overseeing of the windup to the wed-a-thon had demanded most of her time.

Truth to tell, she and Joe had been avoiding each other, from what she could gauge. He'd given her much to think about but very little to act upon. Clearly, he wanted them to have some kind of relationship, but he never spelled out just what direction that might take. A dinner and movie now and again? An exclusive dating arrangement? Something more? Until she knew better what he expected to happen between them, Jenny had chosen the path of least resistance—to wait and do nothing. The ball was in his court. Let him make the first move—again. Meanwhile, she had work to do.

As the last council member scurried off down the hall, Jenny leaned out and called after them, "I know you'll all feel as good about this as I do."

She said it, but she wondered if it could possibly be true. Who here could equal her in excitement over the prospect of a new doctor taking over the clinic? Likely, no one except maybe Doc Hobbs, who'd now be able to retire officially even when Alex had gone back to Kansas City to stay.

"Well, who'd have guessed it?" Joe strolled up to her, his cocky walk typical of his behavior in council meetings since the very first day he covered one for the paper. "You go off to spend a weekend with snooty ol' Alex and make contact with someone interested in coming down here to set up a medical practice."

"Yes, and the new doctor didn't even have us confused with Baxter Springs," she teased. Or was it really teasing? Somehow whenever Joe was around, the things she said and did took on layered meanings, subtleties, nuances that she herself wasn't even aware of until too late.

"That was just an initial mistake on my part." He tucked his pencil behind one ear and stuffed his small writing pad into the back pocket of his jeans. "I figured out where the job really was pretty quick."

"When? Sometime in your first week in town? What gave it away? The absence of phantom cowboys or the presence of great big bronze Bow Boy in town square?" This time she was teasing. She was sure of it. She even found herself laughing good-naturedly at Joe's eye-rolling and head-shaking over her every jab.

"Yeah, yeah. I'm sorry I ever told you that now. It was an easy mistake to make. When the city editor in St. Louis told me the job was in a small town in Kansas on Route 66, I just assumed—"

"Never assume." She wagged a finger at him in warning as she repeated the old newspaper maxim.

"Yeah, yeah. I know. Which brings me to the topic of the new doctor."

"You were here. You heard." She motioned him out of the now empty meeting room. As he stepped into the hallway, she pulled the door shut behind them. The resounding echo of the old door banging shut had hardly died in the deserted hallway when Jenny's heels began a quick-paced clatter as she started to lead Joe out of the building.

"Well, I was here. But I'm not one hundred percent sure I heard." He held his ground. Weight shifted to one hip, one hand tucked into the back of his faded jeans. "In fact, I'd be willing to wager that I did not hear everything there is to hear about this Doctor…Doctor…"

"Dr. Gannon," she supplied through a sugarcoated smile. "What more is there to hear? Good credentials, big debt from medical school. The town helps pay the bills off; we get a doctor guaranteed for the next four years. End of story."

"My journalist's instincts tell me there's more to this than you're telling anyone."

"Journalists have instincts? Does that mean you were born pushy and nosy?" It was a pathetic attempt at diverting the subject, but she figured if anything would throw Joe off the trail, a jab at his professionalism might.

"Intuition then," he corrected himself, following so close behind her she felt the need to rush along, not setting her foot squarely down for fear of having him clip the back of her pump with the toe of his tennis shoe. "Something about the way you handled all this is fishy."

"Gee, Joe, this is Kansas. I thought you believed everything here was corny, not fishy. Are you changing your diet?" She eyed the doorway at the end of the hall. Once she got him outside, down the stairs, and across the street to the We-Do Weddings Chapel, she could hopefully lose him in the chaos of the wedding party departing.

"Nice try, but I'm not changing anything, especially the subject. What's going on, Your Honor? What are you trying to pull?"

"I'm not trying to pull anything, Joe." She braced her hands against the brass bar to open the door. "But I am going to push this door open, and once we're outside I'm off-duty for the evening. You can save any further questions for an official occasion, 'kay?"

He stopped. "So, you're saying, not only are you writing me off socially, you are shutting me out professionally?"

Jenny froze, her fingers curled around the cold metal of the bar on the door. She considered charging on outside and trying to straighten this out later, but she just could not do it. She pivoted to face Joe, one hand still on the door. "I have not written you off socially or any other way. As for shutting you out professionally—it is not my job to tell you every little detail of my agenda, nor do I owe you a point-by-point explanation of everything I do."

"Let's put the personal stuff aside for now, Jenny. You've made it pretty clear that you're not ready to move forward on that issue." He shoved his shirt sleeve up, looking weary and resigned about what he had just told her. Then he cocked his head, narrowed his eyes, and laced his arms tightly over his bedraggled tie. "But it's the job of the press to uncover the details of your agenda, Jenny, especially if there is even a hint that someone in power is withholding information or trying in some way to manipulate the power the voters entrusted her with."

"Manipulate?" The term actually caused a twinge of pain inside her, as much for its meaning as for who had suggested it of her. She lightly rapped her fist on her chest. "Me?"

"What else am I to conclude?" He stuck his large hand out and began ticking things off on his long, blunt fingers. "You called a last-minute meeting on a Friday night when everyone would be anxious to get home or off to other plans."

"I called it now because the doctor is coming to town this weekend for a second visit. I explained that. Dr. Gannon's first visit had proven very pleasant, and in talking with Alex, Nurse Pritchet, Doc Hobbs, and myself, we'd come up with this mutually satisfying proposal. When the doctor called me this afternoon to tell me a schedule change meant the second visit had to happen immediately, I rolled into action. Simple as that."

She snapped her fingers, still keeping one hand on the door. "We needed to approve the financing idea and to get up a committee to conduct the interview, so I called the council meeting ASAP."

"Then why did you first wear everyone down with lengthy information about the wed-a-thon and Labor Day? Going so far as to hype up the final wedding—identical twin sisters marrying identical twin brothers?" He shook his head.

"Oh, I think that's a terrific idea, Joe." She practically bubbled out the words. "Gimmicky, yes, but then gimmicks bring out publicity, don't they?"

"All that stuff could have been handled in any regular

council meeting, Your Honor. Why dwell on it now? Why waste that time letting everyone get anxious and ready to get out of there when you could have gone straight to the new business while everyone was fresh?"

She huffed in exasperation. "Since we were all together tonight anyway, why have two meetings when one would do?"

"That's exactly my question. Why? What are you up to, Jenny?" He peered at her, the fading light of early evening making his features unreadable. But his quiet stance said enough. He wanted answers, and he wasn't budging until he got some.

"You sprang the concept of the new doctor on the council at the very last minute, giving this Dr. Gannon a huge buildup. You went over all manner of professional references, threw in some endorsements by Doc and Alex, peppered the whole thing with a few medical jokes, but in truth you really said very little about Gannon himself. If I had to sum up the overall approach to recommending we interview this doc and seriously consider hiring him, it would be to call your evasive and enthusiastic presentation just another big PR push."

Jenny tensed, causing the brass bar in her hand to rattle. She clenched her teeth, not ready to blurt out the whole truth to Joe and risk ruining her carefully set-up plans. Why did he alone do this to her? Why did he see through her so easily and never let her get away with anything? Why did she find that so endearing and yet impossibly frustrating at the same time? "Land's sake, Joe, why do you have to make everything that goes on between us so complicated?"

"To quote a local politician"—he pounded a fist to his chest—"*Me?* I don't think this is my doing, and besides that, what do you mean *everything* between us? Are we talking personally now too? Could this possibly mean that some of the things I said in Baxter Springs got through to you?"

"See what I mean?" She slapped her hand against her thigh. "Complicated. One minute we're talking doctors, then town business, then you're accusing me of a PR push, then it's on to our personal relationship. Where will this roller-coaster ride take us next, Joe?"

"How about to the truth, Jenny?" He stepped closer to her.

She swallowed, touched her hair, then gripped the door handle more tightly.

"What's the real deal here, Your Honor?" Joe moved in closer still.

Now Jenny could feel the warmth radiating from his skin and smell the clean scent of the summer sun clinging to his cotton dress shirt.

"You're hiding something, and I can tell it." He scanned her face with an intense gaze, then sighed and pulled back. A sly smile quirked his lips up on one side and his brows angled down over the mischievous glint in his eyes. "This guy isn't going to turn out to be another ex-fiancé of yours, is he?"

"Dr. Gannon? Hardly." Jenny laughed, genuinely relieved that the conversation had turned to something so preposterous. "She…uh, I mean Dr. G—"

"She? The new doctor is a *she?*" Joe hooted out a hard, knowing laugh. "Well, no wonder you wanted to save that tidbit until after they'd sent a committee 'round to interview her. You didn't want any of the old guard to work up any pre-conceived notions before they even sat down to meet the lady, right?"

"I'd appreciate it if you wouldn't say anything about it until they do have that meeting." She put one finger to her lips, like a librarian shushing a rowdy kid. "I feel really bad about not being able to have told everyone this up front, but I wanted Dr. Gannon to get a fair shake, and not giving them all the facts seemed the only way to do that."

"You kept your mouth shut because it was the right thing to do. I understand completely."

"Yes, I believe you do." Jenny lowered her gaze.

Joe stuffed his hands in his pockets. "Anyway, since the paper doesn't come out until Thursday and the interview is tomorrow afternoon, you've got nothing to fear from me getting a scoop."

"Good. Thanks." She let out a long breath. "Right now everyone is pumped up about the idea of a new doctor. They'll talk to one another and get more people warmed up to the idea. By the time they meet her, the few people who just might be put off by a young, single female doctor will hopefully be outnumbered by those who see how important it is for our community to keep the clinic open and operating."

"Good thinking, Your Honor. Sneaky, but solid." He tapped one finger to his temple and grinned at her. "That's one of the things I love about you."

Love. Innocently spoken, no great profession of his undying devotion, and yet the momentous word hung in the air between them.

Their gazes locked.

The phrase reverberated in Jenny's mind—*one of the things he loved about her.* Did that mean there were others? Did that mean that in some way—in many ways—Joe was already in love with her? She held her breath.

The joking laughter in Joe's expression faded.

Jenny could hear her pulse thrumming in her ears. She knew she should say something to break the tension or even

Annie Jones

acknowledge Joe's compliment, but her voice deserted her.

Finally Joe scuffed his shoe on the floor, dropped his gaze, and coughed. When he looked up again, it was not at Jenny. "So, when do you suppose I can meet this fabulous new lady doctor?"

"Meet her? Why would you need to meet her?"

"Hello?" He held up an imaginary telephone receiver. "Newspaper editor here. My job is to gather the news of local impact and interest. Just going with my instincts here—no, make that intuition—but the town getting a new doctor, male or female, does seem to fall in that category."

"It's always work with you, isn't it?" She registered disgust at his impatience to get right on the job.

"Said the kettle to the pot," he countered. "Besides, maybe it's not *all* business."

"Oh?" She'd passed up her chance to take this to a personal level at the start of the conversation. She'd missed the excuse to explore the potential of their relationship moments ago when she'd let his use of the *L*-word slide by. Jenny would not let this third opportunity get away from her. "So, you're saying that keeping me here to discuss this new lady doctor isn't necessarily just a business ploy?"

"Not necessarily." He took his pencil from behind his ear and began to tap the eraser in his open palm. "We have had that discussion before about how few interested, unattached young men and women there are in this town."

"Yes?" She wet her lips.

"Well…" He stopped bouncing the pencil and fixed his half-shut eyes on her.

"Well?" she prodded.

"Well, you did say the new lady doctor is single, didn't you?"

Jenny stiffened. "Yes, but—"

204

"Great." He leaned forward.

She braced herself against the cool door. Obviously, he'd teased her enough and finally decided to make his move.

His arm brushed hers as he reached past her.

She tilted her head up, not so much as to seem forward, but just enough so that should he decide to kiss her—

Whoosh. He had pushed down the bar in Jenny's hand, and the heavy door fell open behind her. "If the lady doctor is single, then I guess you could say that doing a story on her may prove to be more than just business after all. Maybe I'll make a point of looking her up this weekend and we can go house hunting together."

Jenny had to stagger to keep from toppling over, but she could not blame the door's backward momentum entirely for the loss of her equilibrium. Joe's abrupt about-face in his attitude toward her had her head positively spinning. "What? House hunting? What are you talking about, Joe?"

"I've decided to buy a house in Cupid's Corner." He paused in front of her, a restlessness evident in his posture and the way his gaze kept darting away. "I may not be able to take some kind of loyalty oath that I'll never leave here, but for now it's my home and it's time I started treating it like that. So, I'm going to start house hunting."

House hunting. It's my home. Joe's sentiments echoed through her. First he'd spoken of loving her, now of his need to make her town his home. It would all be so wonderful, so much more than she could ever have hoped for, if only—

"Joe, what does all this have to do with the new doctor? Why would you want to take her house hunting with you?"

"Hey, she's an outsider. I'm an outsider. What more do I have to say?" He held his arms out. "Sounds like the beginning of a beautiful friendship—or maybe something more."

He had to be joking about this, didn't he? After all the time he'd invested in Jenny, all the feelings he'd awakened in her again, the way he'd had her rethinking her stand on never wanting to leave Cupid's Corner. How could he just walk off and leave her behind, his sights set on getting to know another woman? "B-but you don't even know what she looks like," Jenny protested.

"Looks fade. People change. You can't go by looks; you have to find that common bond, share mutual goals, that kind of thing." He waved his hand in the air. "Besides, it's not like I'm taking her as my mail-order bride. I'm just saying, is all."

"Just saying *what?*"

"Maybe you haven't learned anything from the story of the Cupid statue or the new romance blossoming between Doc and Pritchy, but I sure did. Time's awastin', Jenny, but I'm not wasting any more of it."

"Who said anything about wasting time? I thought you and I had finally reached the point where we—"

"We? What *we?* You turned me down often enough, Your Honor. I got the message. There is no *we,* just you and me—and I'm outta here." He swept past her onto the broad concrete steps outside City Hall.

Jenny stared after him, dumbfounded.

Joe stretched his arms out to his sides, took a deep, noisy breath, then slapped himself on the chest with both hands. She supposed if he'd been a local farmer wearing the basic pair of denim overalls, he'd have hooked his thumbs in the straps and rocked back and forth on the balls of his feet, like a rooster getting ready to crow.

"Yep," he said, turning his head as if scanning from one end of Main Street to the other. "Time is awastin'. Wonder if the new lady doc goes to church? Don't think I could get tangled up with a girl who didn't go to church. Of course, if she doesn't, I could always work on converting her."

With that he started down the steps and out toward the gathering in front of the wedding chapel.

On the chapel steps a couple of young men in ill-fitting tuxedos and young girls in raspberry pink dresses had emerged to announce that the newlyweds were on their way out.

Jenny stood and watched Joe make his way over the lawn and to the street. *There is no we,* he'd said.

Jenny's cheeks stung; her legs and arms felt like lead. She blinked and unleashed a wash of hot tears that blurred her vision. Still, she watched the man she'd come to count on, to laugh with, to argue with, to…love—

Yes, as she watched him leaving her, Jenny finally had the nerve to admit it. She loved Joe Avery. She probably had for a long time. And now he was marching out of her life, away from any chance of a lasting relationship, because she had chased him away forever with her stubbornness and insecurity.

Her teeth sank into her lower lip. She sniffled. She wanted to call out after him but had no idea what she would say to him, and so she said the only thing she knew she could depend on, even when her heart was breaking—a prayer for guidance.

Please, Lord, show me what to do. Help to clear my mind so that I can open my heart and do what's best for both Joe and me. I love him, Lord, and I believe that he could—that he does—love me. I have to find the way to bridge the gap between us. Please, give me the strength to do what I should have done a long time ago—to take the risk of getting hurt in exchange for finding happiness.

She opened her eyes and scanned the busy street for any

sign of Joe. She saw the Cupid statue gleaming in the golden rays of the setting sun. She saw a small but exuberant group milling around the chapel, waiting for the bride and groom to come out and present themselves. She saw Doc and Nurse Pritchet strolling hand in hand along the sidewalk. She found Joe standing, his back to her, near the steps of the chapel. He checked his watch, glanced up at the chapel doors, then checked his watch again.

"Time's awastin'," she murmured as she drew up her shoulders, took a deep breath of fresh evening air, and headed down the steps of City Hall. "But I'm not wasting any more of it either."

❧ ❧

It took every bit of control for Joe to keep from looking back at Jenny as he strode across the lush lawn of City Hall.

Him and the lady doctor? Yeah, right! Maybe in twenty or thirty years from now, when he'd finally given up all hope of ever winning Jenny Fox over, *maybe*. Until then—well, he allowed himself a chuckle to think that merely suggesting he might look elsewhere for romance made Jenny so jealous it struck her speechless.

Speechless! Jenny! He could chuckle over that, but he would not look back. He couldn't.

He crossed the street, feigning interest in the proceedings at the quaint wedding chapel. He thought of the first wedding he and Jenny had come to here this summer, the one with the nervous groom. He remembered how badly he had wanted to impress her then, how much he had tried to play things safe, not wanting to scare her off. He thought of how he had almost kissed her that night, when she'd lunged into his arms after backing into the statue of Cupid. He thought if he ever had another opportunity like that one, he wouldn't let it pass him by.

No, he'd be taking a different approach from here on out. He had played things her way long enough. Maybe now that she thought he'd reached his limit, she'd understand that he wouldn't be dangled on the line indefinitely. Maybe now she'd know what it felt like to him when Alex Michaels had arrived, and she had acted as if she were seeing her old flame in a whole new light. Maybe now that he'd stopped letting her treat him like a security blanket—always around when she needed him, but easily tucked out of sight at her convenience—it wouldn't take those twenty or thirty years for something to get started between them.

"Joe Avery, if you think I am going to let you just walk away on that note, then I'm afraid you've got another think coming."

Maybe it would only take twenty or thirty seconds. Joe straightened, turning only his head in profile. Still, from the corner of his eye he could see Jenny, her windswept brunette hair flashing around her flushed cheeks as she drew closer to him. The sight made him want to laugh and cheer at the same time. It made him want to run to her, grab her up in his arms, and…and he knew better than to try any of those things.

Much as his heart wanted to hope otherwise, his mind knew he had taken this ride before. Jenny might well have charged over here thinking she'd just take back control of the situation and things would go on as they had been between them.

"Another think coming?" He scowled. "What does that mean?"

"It means if you think you can throw out this idea that you want to see someone else, that it might just be too late for us before we ever even got our relationship on solid ground, then you have some serious rethinking to do."

She reached the bottom of the chapel steps where he stood. "After all the time you spent pursuing me? Then just when you finally help me start to get my priorities straight, you want to walk away from it all now? No sir, I don't think so. Not without a fight."

"I don't want to fight with you, Jenny," he said softly, his heart soaring.

"I don't want to fight *with* you either, Joe." She did not take his lead and lower her voice. "But I will fight *for* you; I'll fight for us."

"Shh, Jenny. People are starting to stare," he warned. Though he couldn't have cared less if the whole world looked on, he knew she'd regret making a scene once she calmed down and reflected back on what she'd done. "Maybe we should just go back—"

"I don't want to go anywhere until you tell me what you're thinking."

He took her by the elbow, trying to guide her back toward City Hall and the privacy of her office. "I'm thinking maybe you should either tone it down or take it back to—"

"The only thing I want to take back, Joe, is how hard I've been on you." She placed her hands on his chest and refused to budge. "Tell me you forgive me for all my stubbornness. Tell me you haven't really given up on us. Just tell me what you feel, Joe."

"You want me to tell you how I feel?"

She nodded slowly, her eyes solemn.

He drew in a deep breath, taking in the scent of her gentle floral perfume and shutting out the sights and sounds all around them. The only thing he saw, the only thing he knew, was that Jenny was finally in his arms, and not by some fluke or because she was tired and overwrought. She'd come to him. After all the months they'd circled one another without any real progress, she had come to him. He would not let another moment slip by.

"You want to know how I feel?" He wrapped his arms around her.

"Tell me," she murmured.

"How about I show you instead?" He saw the flicker in her eyes that said she knew what he intended and she approved. So he lowered his head over hers, pulled her tightly to him, and kissed her.

Whether it took a few seconds or a few minutes, Joe had no idea. So completely lost was he in the moment, in the joy of having Jenny in his embrace, of kissing her and having her kiss him back, that time meant nothing. He could stay here indefinitely.

A cheer of approval from the crowd around them brought them to their senses, making them aware of where they were and how many eyes focused on them.

Joe ended the kiss.

Jenny pulled away, gave him a shy glance, then stepped away.

Just then the new bride and groom appeared at the door of the wedding chapel and another cheer erupted.

Jenny put her hand to her cheek. "I thought all that commotion was for us."

"You'd reckon the newspaper editor and the mayor kissing in broad daylight would attract at least a little attention." Joe laughed.

"I guess they're all preoccupied with…" Her voice trailed off as she paused and looked toward the happy couple at the top of the stairs.

The couple waved.

Several camera flashes illuminated the dusky, early summer evening sky.

The couple kissed.

More flashes.

More kisses.

Joe moved to stand directly behind Jenny. He placed one hand on her waist and caused her silky hair to flutter when he whispered into her ear, "What are you thinking, Jenny? That that could be us someday soon?"

"Us? Like…them?" She blinked. She blushed bright red from her collarbone to her forehead. "Soon? No!"

He chuckled. "Why not? We've known each other eight months now. I'm crazy about you, and you're obviously just plain crazy. You'd have to be, to be as head-over-heels about me as you seem."

"Lunatics in love." She moaned out a melodramatic sigh as the newlywed couple descended the steps. "Isn't it a beautiful thing?"

The woman standing next to them gave them a stern look.

Joe burst out laughing.

Jenny flushed an even deeper shade of red than before, if that was possible. "No, I meant him and me, not the bride and groom! Honestly, I wasn't calling them lunatics, ma'am, I was calling myself one—"

"And proving your point by babbling on about it," Joe cautioned. He offered a clenched smile to the woman standing next to Jenny, whose opinion had only worsened, judging from the sour expression on her face.

"She's going to toss the bouquet!" someone called out from the wedding party.

"Maybe we should just get out of here," Jenny whispered.

A cluster of girls in pastel dresses began to move. They shifted to the right, their arms raised overhead.

"Are you trying to make your getaway without answering my question?" Joe held her in her place.

She wriggled in his grasp. "Joe, it's so sudden. It's so unexpected. We just agreed a few minutes ago to have a relationship, and now you're talking marriage? Don't you think that's moving just a little too fast?"

The bride lifted her bouquet in both hands. A few feet away from Jenny and Joe, the gaggle of girls on the sidewalk squealed in delighted anticipation of the bride's throw.

"I wasn't asking you to set a date, Jenny." He stood firm. He'd been down this hurry-up-and-wait trail before, so he knew she hadn't just been buying herself time but was still intending to avoid any real commitment. "I'm only asking if you think that's where this thing between us is headed."

"Oh, Joe, it's all so new. How can I give you a well-thought-out answer now?"

"I've got it!" an exuberant bridesmaid screamed.

"No, I do!" another announced.

"You knocked it out of my hands!" the first one accused just seconds before the whole knot of young women became a flurry of swishing dresses, swaying hands, and arms flailing to snag the big bundle of white ribbon and pink roses that had dropped into their midst.

"Then when can you give me some kind of answer?" he pressed.

"I don't know. Not anytime soon."

"Why doesn't that surprise me?" He stepped away from her, shoving his hands into his pockets.

"Oh, don't act that way, Joe. Really! This isn't some personal affront, it's merely a case of bad timing."

" 'Twas ever thus," he muttered.

"Be reasonable, Joe. I've got the new doctor's interview to think about, all the plans and meetings for the summer's big event finale, arrangements for extra publicity and all that entails." She turned on her heel with a flounce and took one step toward the street.

Joe moved in behind her, determined to see this through.

"Frankly, the last thing I have on my mind right now is—"

"It's going to land in the street, somebody catch it!" the bride warned in a high-pitched plea.

Jenny turned just in time to prevent the hurtling floral arrangement from smacking up alongside her head. In one clearly unintentional but fluid movement, she opened her arms and raised her hands.

Joe opened his mouth, more in shock than to say anything significant. He thought of reaching over Jenny and safely batting the thing away from her but realized he'd probably knock her over in the process. Besides, who ever heard of anyone sustaining lasting injury from catching the bride's bouquet?

Jenny leaned forward, getting under the thing like a baseball player ready to sacrifice herself to capture a fly ball.

Joe stood back and watched it all happen like a slow-motion moment in a screwball comedy, though in reality it only took a split second.

Then the bridal bouquet landed in Jenny's arms with a crisp rustle of lace, a heavy thud, and a spattering of moisture from the depths of the stems just as she concluded her pronouncement for Joe that the *last thing I have on my mind right now is* "—marriage."

*...Speak now,
or forever hold
your peace.*

—*request made in marriage ceremony*

Thirteen

August 27

Won't she make a beautiful bride?"
"And what about him? Have you ever seen a happier bridegroom?"

Jenny took Joe's arm, nodded, and made chitchat with the other wedding guests at First Methodist Church for Larry Hackerman's little sister's wedding. Great swooping swells of organ music carried from the sanctuary into the outer room where they stood, waiting to be seated by the ushers. White and pink ribbons, flowers, and flocked doves holding red hearts adorned absolutely everything around them, setting the scene for the kind of affair tailor-made for a town called Cupid's Corner.

Practically everyone in town was here too—which made Jenny far more tense than she might otherwise have been.

"So, our first really big town event as a couple," Joe remarked as he raised his hand in greeting to the high school football coach across the way. "Think anyone's going to make a big deal?"

"Oh no, I don't see why they would." It was wishful thinking and Jenny knew it. Still, she prattled cheerfully on, her fingers curled into Joe's jacket sleeve in a white-knuckled death grip. "We've been officially dating for ten whole days now. They've all noticed us sharing every lunch hour with each other and taking walks around the square in the evenings. So it's not like seeing us here together now will seem like any big deal to anyone, right?"

"Exactly. Why should the two of us draw any attention today? Just two ordinary people. A pretty young lady mayor—nothing unusual there—and your standard tall, dark, and handsome newspaper editor out arm in arm at the most romantic wedding of the whole romance-saturated summer."

Jenny stole a peek at Joe through half-lowered lashes.

"We're just two average folks who happened to be notorious around town for their squabbles and square-offs—with the notable exception of what many people still believe to be a passionate embrace on the Fourth of July—"

"I stumbled!" She gave his arm a playful shake. "You know I did."

"You were pushed," he corrected, raising his eyebrows.

"Pushed?"

"By Cupid."

"I thought that Cupid shot his arrows through your heart. I got mine a little farther south."

Joe shook his head. "You were a particularly stubborn case, my dear. I think Bow Boy had to get at you any way he could."

The man made her laugh. He made the troubles of her job and the intrusiveness of small-town life all fade away. He meant more to her than she knew how to express, certainly more than she had told him.

She knew it now. She loved Joe Avery. She just had no idea how to let him know that without risking his rejection. This was her problem, not his, and she knew it.

In her mind, she saw no reason to think Joe would ever do anything to hurt her, but her heart...well, it had been fooled before and she just wasn't quite ready to lay it out there. It had taken her enough time to overcome her confusion and reticence after she lost Alex the first time; if she lost Joe, she wondered if she would ever recover.

For now, though, she'd just savor the blossoming relationship and do her best to totally blot out any teasing, speculation, or outright gossip their being together might spark, starting with enjoying the service. They moved forward in the crowd of people outside the sanctuary. Now they could see the satin-covered aisle and the altar all done up in tulle, flowers, and candles.

The sight made Jenny feel all warm and optimistic. Someday, maybe, if her prayers and dreams were answered, she would be standing there, a bride, with Joe as her groom. Though she had no interest in a fancy production like this one, she could imagine herself standing before a minister, or maybe even the chaplain at the We-Do Weddings Chapel, taking her vows with the man she loved in a simple but meaningful ceremony. Her anxieties eased about the two of them getting teased and goaded to disclose more about their relationship. Someday everyone would know exactly how they felt about each other. Someday—maybe soon.

She leaned in close to Joe to whisper, "What am I worried about? This is the wedding couple's big day. Who would even give us a second thought? What with all the decorations, the excitement, the whole love-and-marriage-and-happily-ever-after atmosphere, who on earth would even care about our new relationship? We're totally inconsequential. We're—"

"You're next."

Jenny turned to find Larry grinning down at her like the

cat who ate the canary—or maybe the Cupid who ate the wedding cake.

"Larry Hackerman, you take that back right now, or I won't need my sister to come here and make you do it. *Next? We're next?*" She tried to laugh at the boldly ill-timed joke, more startling on the heels of her daydream of some-day marrying Joe. "For heaven's sake, Joe and I just came to the wedding together, that's all there is to it. That's hardly a reason to assume that he and I would be the next ones get-ting married!"

Larry blinked at her.

Joe put his lips close to her ear and pointed to their friend's outstretched arm. "He meant we're next to be seated for the wedding. Larry is an usher, Jen."

"Oh." She managed a faint smile, then slipped her arm in Larry's and let him lead her down the aisle to a seat on the bride's side of the church.

"Nooo, sir. No, nope, nope, nope, no, no," Joe muttered under his breath for only her to hear as he settled in beside her. "Not going to draw any attention to ourselves today, are we?"

Jenny felt bad. Not embarrassed because she overre-acted. She sort of had a way of doing that, especially lately, with the stress of the summer's events and the tension of try-ing to handle all the changes in a life that resisted change for so long. No, she felt bad.

One moment she had been wondering how she would ever get up the nerve to tell Joe she loved him, how she would survive if he did not love her back. Then she'd even stopped to daydream about their own marriage. The next thing she knew she was practically denying their whole rela-tionship. She had to find a way to make it up to him. She had to find a way to let him—and everyone nosy enough to want to know—that she cared about Joe and cared deeply. It could not wait for some fictitious someday. She had to act today.

❧   ❧

The bride was beautiful. The groom—well, kind of goofy and gawky but filled with pride and the kind of happiness that only comes when the girl of your dreams promises to love you forever. Joe had sat through the ceremony, trying not to relate the words of the vows, the sentiments of the songs, and the mood of the moment to his relationship with Jenny. Clearly that would be jumping to a conclusion that was anything but certain.

If he were a wise man, and he wasn't entirely sure that he was, he'd back off, play it cool. He'd pushed Jenny all summer long. Pushed her since the day he'd first met her and thought what a strong, amazing, sometimes high-strung, but decent-to-the-core woman she was. Now he needed to let her set the pace.

"So, you want to skip out on the reception and go driving along Route 66 to see if we can round up some lost cowboys' ghosts or maybe just some stray lovers looking for a place to elope?" He slid his hands around her waist as they blended in with the other guests making the short walk from the church to the wedding chapel, the only place with a hall big enough for this party.

Her soft hair brushed his cheek as she glanced over her shoulder to meet his gaze. She smiled.

That was enough for Joe. He knew she'd never shirk her responsibilities to community and constituents and ditch the big town-wide doings. But her impish smile, hinting that she was actually considering his offer, made his heart light.

"You think anyone would miss us?"

"Are you…are you kidding, Jenny? You might actually do it?" He tightened his grasp on her, slowing them both down a bit so that others began to pass by them. "Miss Everybody-expects-this-of-me-and-I-can't-let-them-down? You might play hooky from this thing? Knowing it could cause some folks to talk, to speculate about how serious we're getting?"

"Well, there's something important I want to tell you, and you know what they say, Joe."

Just then Doc and Pritchy strolled by hand in hand, oblivious to everyone around them.

She maneuvered around so that they, too, could walk openly hand in hand. "Time's awastin'."

He pulled up short and let the others make their way around the two of them. Leaning in, he placed the lightest of kisses on her sweet lips.

And to his surprise and delight, she let him.

When he straightened away, she batted her lashes up at him and spoke in a soft, most unmayorly tone. "Well, I guess if people weren't going to speculate before, they will now, Joe Avery. Because in this little corner of Kansas, we don't go around kissing just anybody for just any reason."

"Is that so?" He crooked his knuckle under her chin.

"Oh yes. For a town with such a romantic-sounding name, we're pretty funny about who we let get away with public displays of affection. We pretty much reserve those for—"

"Jenny! Joe! You two, wait up," Alex Michaels called from behind a family herding seemingly countless children down the sidewalk.

"If you want to, we can still make a run for it," Joe suggested, only half kidding.

"No." Jenny stood firm and crossed her arms. "I am through running from the specter of Alex, once and for all."

Though he'd known that Doctor Deceitful had been out of the picture but good ever since her disastrous trip to Kansas City, Jenny's simple proclamation made Joe's heart soar.

"Hey, you two. I sat a few rows behind you at the wedding and was hoping I'd catch up with you." The doctor pulled up short, winded from the quick sprint over to where they stood. He gave Joe a passing nod, then fixed his attention on Jenny. "It's good to see you, Jenny. I've been so busy with school physicals and immunization clinics and preseason football injuries, I haven't had the chance to really talk to you since…"

Joe moved to wedge one shoulder protectively between Jenny and the doctor with the expensive suit and the brandnew condo in Kansas City.

"We all know since when," Joe said.

"Jenny, I really owe you an apology. I never should have lied to you."

"No, you shouldn't have," she said with quiet conviction.

"I just…I thought…well, something in me wanted to go back and fix things between us. I wanted a second chance."

"You wanted a second chance to do the same thing all over again—to try to get me to give up the things I care about for the things you crave."

Guilt crossed the doctor's expression for only a moment before he shrugged and let out a resigned but good-natured chuckle. "To think, I came back here expecting to find that same naive little girl I left standing in a toilet-paper wedding dress on the front porch two years ago."

"Toilet-paper what?" Joe twisted his head to lock his gaze on her over his shoulder.

She just shook her head in a gesture clearly intended for both of them. "In some ways you did find her, Alex. She was still here because she never got the chance to grow up. By hanging on to my past hurts and losing myself in my work, I didn't give that heartbroken young girl much hope to mature and move on. This summer I think I finally have."

"Which? Mature or move on?" Alex asked.

"Both." She placed her hand lightly on Joe's arm. "That's why I can accept your apology, Alex, and wish you all the best in your new life—"

"And your new home," Joe added, as if the man needed the reminder that he was now the outsider.

"Same to you, Jenny." Alex leaned toward her, his intentions unmistakable.

Joe intervened, grabbing the doctor's right hand in his own in what he hoped would look like a forceful but friendly handshake from the victor to the vanquished. "Oh no, you don't. In this little corner of Kansas we don't go kissing just anybody out in public."

"Not to worry, Avery. I wasn't going to kiss you." Michaels returned the handshake with equal vigor, his jaw tight but his smile never waning.

When they released their grips, both men stood back a step and gave their hands a brisk shake to let the blood start circulating again. Then Michaels grinned and slapped Joe hard on the back. "Okay, then you kiss her for me." He gave Jenny a tender look that lasted just a few seconds before he touched her cheek and said, "Good-bye, and try to be happy here."

"I'll do even better than that, Alex." She lifted her chin, then shifted her eyes to catch Joe's gaze. "I'll try to be happy *wherever* I am."

Joe wanted to leap in the air and give some kind of primitive whoop of triumph. He wanted to do the kind of idiotic but incredibly cool victory dance that football players did after a touchdown. He wanted…

He turned to see Jenny beaming at him.

He wanted to spend the rest of his life with this woman, knowing that every day he'd feel just like he did right now. He pulled her into a hug that he wished would never end, but he let go after only a moment, remembering his plan not to rush her with too much too fast. "Still want to skip out on the reception?"

She nodded.

He glanced around. Much of the crowd had gone inside, but the photographer and most of the wedding party and their families were gathered nearby, making use of the afternoon light for group pictures. "We can't just turn around and walk off, right here in front of all these people, Jenny."

She slipped her hand in his, and it felt like a perfect fit. "Then we'll just go inside. You know how many halls and back ways this chapel has, Joe. I guess it wouldn't be the worst thing if you and I were to wander down one and find ourselves out the back door, now would it?"

"No, not the worst thing at all." He laughed. "Have I ever told you that this sneaky streak of yours is one of the things I love about you, Jenny?"

"As a matter of fact, you have." She led the way up the chapel stairs and immediately down a side hallway. When they were alone in the darkened passageway, she stopped and turned. "And have I ever told you what I love about you, Joe?"

He took her in his arms. "What?"

"Everything," she whispered.

"Jenny, are you saying…?"

"I love you, Joe Avery."

"I love you too, Jenny," he whispered back, though he hardly knew where he got the breath to answer, feeling the wind knocked out of his sails but good at her wonderful, unbelievable news.

She buried her face between his shoulder and neck and sighed. "You don't know how glad I am to hear you say that."

"Oh, I think I have some idea." He held her close and kissed her temple. "I guess the question now is—"

"Where do we go from here?" She flattened her hands to his chest and did not look at him.

We barge into the chapel and demand somebody marry us immediately if not sooner, he wanted to say. But his decision to take it slow, at Jenny's pace, not to push it, came back to haunt him. Saying "I love you" was not the same as being ready to take a marriage vow on the spot. Jenny had just finally said good-bye to the pain of her past; it would be unreasonable and unfair of him to try to ramrod her into vowing the rest of her future to him at this moment.

He pulled away and lifted her face up so he could give her a grin and say, "Where do we go from here? Cruisin' Route 66. Where else?"

**Cupid's Corner, Kansas, a.k.a. Hitchin' City, USA,
The Elopement Capital of Route 66,
To Set New Record—66 Weddings in 58 Days!**

With the double wedding of identical twin sisters Laurel Ann and Lurlene Overton of Baxter Springs to identical twin brothers Jason and Mason Pellard of Galena, Cupid's Corner, Kansas, will reach its record-breaking goal on Saturday, September 1. The wedding will take place at the We-Do Weddings Chapel at 1 P.M. The press is invited to both the ceremony and the daylong celebration, which includes a parade, a watermelon-seed spitting contest, various food vendors, crafts booths, and games and activity booths sponsored by local churches, organizations, and schools to raise funds for their worthy causes.

—press release sent out by the mayor's office

Fourteen

"What do you mean there isn't going to be any wedding?" Joe rounded the paper-strewn desk in Jenny's office and placed his hands on her shoulders. The tips of his strong fingers dug into her knotted muscles to try to loosen some of the day's tensions even as he lowered his voice to his best soothing tone and laughed. "So Lurlene and Jason ran off last night and are going to get married in the place they had planned to spend their honeymoon. So what? That still leaves Laurel Ann and Mason—"

"So what? Have you seen the crowds in town today? Visitors and regional celebrities. Our new doctor is here with her friends and family. Oh, and speaking of family, my parents, Bobbie Ann, Mark, and the baby all came into town to help me celebrate the conclusion of my first really big project."

"Sounds nice."

"Sounds like my worst nightmare," she corrected, her heart sinking. "Don't you see? I have media from the whole tri-state area here to cover the momentous occasion of our town marking its sixty-sixth wedding in fifty-eight days. Now *this* has happened—"

Jenny dropped her head in her hands and tried to give herself over to Joe's tender ministrations. With all that was going on these last few days they'd hardly had time for more than stolen moments over working lunches and late-night coffee breaks. Still, Jenny treasured every minute she spent with him. And that only confirmed to her that if he would ever ask her again, she would jump at the chance to become his wife. Though the way he avoided the opportunity on the day she told him she loved him had her wondering if all her reluctance had left him gun-shy about ever popping the question in earnest.

The reminder of marriage snapped Jenny's thoughts to the problem at hand. For now the subject of whether she and Joe would ever tie the knot had to take a backseat. It was someone else's wedding woes that had her shoulders tight as iron bands and her head throbbing.

"So let me get this straight." Joe kneaded the base of her taut neck with the heel of his hand. "You're all worked up because, even though the town has completely shattered its old wedding record, the people sent here to cover the story will only see one wedding, which is one wedding shy of the sixty-six mark?"

"Nooo." She wrung the word out between her teeth, more anguished than angry. "I'm all worked up because no one is going to be witnessing any wedding at all!"

"But only one couple ran off, Jenny. That doesn't mean the other couple has to cancel their ceremony."

"It does if the couple that ran off were engaged to the two people left behind," she groaned.

"You mean—" His hands stilled.

"Laurel Ann was supposed to marry Jason and Lurlene was *supposed* to be Mason's bride, but Lurlene ran off with Jason last night, leaving the other two nothing but a note and a bill for the weddings that will not be." Jenny sat back in her chair, giving Joe's hand a pat to thank him for trying to help her unwind. "So instead of a double wedding today, all I have to give the press is an irritating tale of a double dose of the old double cross."

"Boy, I'd hate to be around at that next family reunion."

"Don't try to make me laugh," she warned. "I am not in the mood."

"That bad, huh?"

"Joe, you are looking at a woman who actually considered trying to convince two jilted people that since they were all identical twins anyway, maybe they should take a page from their siblings' playbooks and just go ahead and marry each other."

"Jenny, you wouldn't have!" He chuckled to prove he didn't believe her claim.

"Of course not." She settled back until her chair gave out a long creak. "What would have been the use? We'd still have been one wedding short."

He stopped halfway around her desk and glanced back at her.

"Kidding. I'm just kidding." She rustled around some of the stacks of paper cluttering the desktop. "Still, I wish I had something better to give the press and the public today than that sorry story. After all, they came to see a wedding."

"And who says they can't still see one?"

Jenny blinked. The serious expression on Joe's face did not dissolve into a teasing grin. She rose from her seat and, despite the sudden flux of feelings surging through her, managed to ask, "What did you just say, Joe?"

"I said, if everybody wants a wedding, why don't we see if we can give them one?"

"Oh, Joe I...I...that's so sweet of you to suggest it, since you know how much this means to me and all. And, of course, under any other circumstances my answer would be an unequivocal yes, but..."

"But…?" he urged quietly.

Yes! she wanted to scream. *I'll marry you!*

She'd given him another chance when he'd pretended to walk out on her the day the new doctor first came to town. Now he had given her a second chance at the question she had so longed to hear from him. Still, as much as she longed to throw her arms around him and agree to walk down the aisle with him this very day, she just couldn't do it. She had to be fair to him, to both of them. "But I can't let you do that, Joe. I can't let anyone think that we'd get married just for a publicity stunt. It wouldn't be a stunt for us, of course, but people might think that."

"Married? Us?" He scowled. "Who said anything about us getting married?"

She sank back into her seat, slowly, her wild emotions suddenly numbed as she saw Joe's reaction. "Isn't that what you meant?"

"Actually, I was thinking more like Doc Hobbs and Pritchy." He straightened his tie to the left, then to the right, then jerked it up but not quite enough to get it neatly arranged at his collar. He began to pace the length of her desk, never quite looking her directly in the eye as he went on. "You know they were going to take their vows in the chapel later this month with the whole town looking on anyway. I thought maybe if you and I went to them and explained what's happened and how everybody they want at their wedding will already be primed for a big ceremony this afternoon, maybe we could persuade them to—"

Suddenly he stopped, pivoted around to face her and held up both his hands. "Wait a minute. Did you just say 'yes'?"

"Well, I…" She lifted her chin and pushed her hair behind one ear. "Apparently I misunderstood the question."

"Oh no. You are not going to politician your way out of this one, Your Honor." He moved swiftly around the desk, swiveling her chair to put them face to face when he dropped on one knee in front of her. "I distinctly heard you say your answer would be an 'unequivocal yes.'"

"How can that be my answer, Joe, when evidently you never even asked me a question?" Her lip trembled, but she hoped he did not notice it. This whole mess was embarrassing enough without adding a crying jag to it.

"But if I did ask you…" He let the rest go unsaid, leaving it somewhere between a question and a gentle prod for her affirmation.

"I don't want you to feel like you have to ask, like we'd have to rush this if you're not really ready—not to save my publicity event, of all things," she managed to eke out without her voice breaking.

"Of all things," he repeated with a grin. "When have I ever done *anything* just for the sake of your publicity event?"

Slowly, as she realized the truth of his words and the implication beneath them, Jenny's heart lightened and her smile grew. "Never."

"And so your answer is?"

"And so your *question* is?"

"Jenny Fox, will you marry me? Today?"

"Joe Avery…I will!"

❧   ❧

At one o'clock that afternoon weddings sixty-five and sixty-six of the Record-Breaking Hitchin' City, USA, Wed-A-Thon went off perfectly. The brides, in borrowed gowns, looked absolutely radiant. The grooms, both a little more nervous than they wanted anyone to know, got through the vows with nary a stutter or a cough.

And later that evening when the press and dignitaries and most of the tourists had all gone home, the couples and the loved ones they had near them that day gathered at the Wholly Macaroni Pasta Emporium to celebrate.

Joe, who had not been able to wipe the grin from his face since Jenny had accepted his proposal, raised a glass of iced tea to make a toast. "A little more than a couple of months ago, when we were talking about this project and questioning the probability of getting sixty-six couples to take their marriage vows in Cupid's Corner this summer, we challenged our mayor. We asked her if she would be willing to sacrifice for the cause and get married if there weren't enough weddings to reach the goal. She rose to that challenge and told her entire town council, distinguished guests, and the local newspaper editor just what they could do with the whole idea of marriage."

A murmur of laughter and agreement worked through the crowd.

"She told us we could keep the notion to ourselves. She wanted no part of it. A lot's happened since then." He looked down into her eyes.

"You can say that again," she whispered, answering his gaze with pure adoration.

"I *could* say that again, but this is our wedding night and I'd rather not waste any more time going over old material." He brushed his thumb over her cheek. "Instead, I want to say that, despite my reservations, the event Jenny promoted for so long has accomplished everything she hoped for and more. It's gained recognition for the town, stimulated the economy, helped bring in a new doctor..."

"And made me look at my goals and dreams in a whole new light," Jenny added softly.

"And it hasn't exactly been a bad influence on romance," Joe said.

"Hear, hear!" Doc chimed in, planting a kiss on his new bride's cheek.

Joe acknowledged the other newlyweds with his raised glass. "I just wanted to go on record right now as saying how proud I am of Jenny as our mayor."

A smattering of applause punctuated Joe's sentiment.

"How pleased I am with her work this summer on behalf of all of us."

This time the applauding group threw in a few mumbled cheers.

"And how truly blessed I am to have her as the love of my life, my wife." He took a sip of his tea.

Others followed suit.

Jenny gave them a nod of thanks for their support, then turned to Joe and threw her arms around him. "Thank you so much for that wonderful toast. Shall I make one to you too? I think I can probably come up with a few words of praise for the man I'm going to spend the rest of my life with."

"Kind of you to offer, Mrs. Avery, but if you start naming off all my good qualities, we could be here a very long time, and you know my new motto—"

"Time's awastin'" she said in unison with him.

Joe grinned.

Jenny's knees went weak. Lucky for her, she had someone to lend her support, someone she knew she could always depend on. She tightened her arms around Joe and kissed him as she had never kissed any man before in her life—as a happily married woman.

If you enjoyed Cupid's Corner, *check out Annie Jones's* The Double Heart Diner. *The following is an excerpt from the first book in Annie Jones's Route 66 Series, available in bookstores now.*

The diner wasn't as forbidding or gloomy a place as he'd expected. On the contrary, with its chrome and mirrors and ribbon of neon color that flowed along the top of the walls in one unending wave, it seemed to bid him welcome. A big jukebox—the kind that looked like it still played records, though it clearly advertised it featured CDs—stood at one end of the building, like the guardian of some portal to the past.

None of the handful of patrons sitting at the booths even looked up when he entered, nor did the lone man, dressed all in black, sitting hunched at the end of the long lunch counter.

Jett breathed in the aroma of slap-in-the-face-strong coffee brewing and cheeseburgers frying. And onion rings. He sniffed again. And…what was that other smell? He couldn't quite identify it.

He thought of the splintered-wood-and-natural-stone sign, beside the road about a half-mile back, that had once encouraged tourists to stop at the diner by promising "We put a Double helping of Heart in every serving!" Someone, years ago by the look of it, had carved an addition, big and bold, so that the board now read: "We put a Double helping of Heart*burn* in every serving."

Jett took another deep breath and needed nothing more

than the smell of the food to convince him of the correction's accuracy. Not that he would mind a good case of heartburn. It sure had heart*ache* beat by a mile. If he could forget that miserable feeling, even for a little while, that would do him just fine. He took a seat and tried not to look at the silver-haired man—the *prematurely* silver-haired man, he corrected himself—looking back at him from the mirror.

The cook, visible through a pair of swinging doors propped open, slapped another burger on the old-style grill. Jett watched as he pressed down hard with his narrow spatula until grease oozed out around the edges, hissing and popping.

Might as well order himself one of those, he thought. Flipping open the menu, he searched for what he expected could most aptly be named "The Double Heart Attack on a Platter."

"Why, hi, sweet-thing. I don't believe I've ever seen you in here before." Jett looked up as a waitress, with black hair that looked as if it had been inflated by a tire pump, stuck her hand across the counter. "Starla Mae Jenkins at your service, sassy waitress with a heart of gold—and they ain't a dime a dozen. Remember that when figuring your tip, now. And you are…?"

Jett sniffed the air. "Bubblegum."

The waitress cocked her head at him. "How's that again?"

"The smell. A minute ago, I was trying to figure out what it was. I just realized: It's bubblegum." He laughed to himself. "I knew it was familiar. I just couldn't quite put my finger on it."

"Oh, now, you don't want to go and do that."

"Do what?"

"Put your finger on my bubblegum." She blinked at him as if he was a total idiot, then blew a small bubble and let it pop pale pink against her bright red lips.

"No, I…that is…" Jett sighed and shut his eyes, feeling worn down without having actually done anything. "So, you're Starla Mae Jenkins, huh? You're not exactly what I expected. Or maybe you're everything I expected and then some."

Starla Mae laughed. It was a far more amiable laugh than he had expected would come out of someone who, he happened to know, worked hard just to scrape by as owner of this nearly bankrupt diner. He liked the sound of it, warm and genuine. "And you're…?"

Jett paused. "Does the name 'Padgett Group' mean anything to you?"

"Ahhh," Starla smacked her gum again. "So you've come to see the place for yourself then?"

So he had, but not for the reasons she'd suspect. He looked at Starla for a long moment. His stomach grumbled. "Can we postpone talk about business for a while? I've been driving all day and haven't eaten. What I'd really like to do now is just order."

"Nobody 'just orders' at the Double Heart Diner, sweet-thing. Ain't that right, y'all?"

One man at a booth by the window grunted agreement while another customer mumbled his support. The fellow at the end of the counter took his time to straighten, then made a half-spin on his stool, faced Jett, and curled his lip up in a snarl. His eyes were hooded as he growled a husky "That's right, darlin'."

Jett let the menu in his hands fall to the countertop. "That…that looks like—"

"Yep." Starla leaned closer. "The ghost of Elvis. He haunts the Double Heart Diner on lonely summer nights like these. Just sits there all alone at the end of the counter until a stranger, like you, spots him and then…"

"And then?" Jett didn't believe a word of it, but he found himself drawn in by Starla Mae's intense, sparkling eyes and hushed tone.

"Pffft."

"Pffft?"

Starla Mae snapped her fingers, setting off a ripple effect that had her bracelets clattering. "He's gone—leaving nothing but the key to a pink Cadillac and the footprints of his blue suede shoes."

"Huh?" Jett knew his mouth was hanging open, but he couldn't seem to make it stay shut.

Starla Mae grinned. "And if you swallow that, let me get you one of our twenty-dollar milkshakes to wash it down with."

"Twenty dollars?" Jett blinked, then it all fell into place for him and he joined the waitress in a "gotcha" chuckle.

"Elvis, hon, come on over here and be sociable." She motioned to the man in black, who slid down until only one stool separated him from Jett. "This is my baby brother, Elvis—"

"You mean he impersonates Elvis," Jett ventured, still trying to make sense of what he was seeing and hearing.

"*Young* Elvis," the man emphasized.

"Yes, he does impersonate him. And quite well too. It's just one of his many, many talents." Starla Mae beamed with pride. "And his name happens to be Elvis, as well. Ain't that a hoot?"

"You took the words right out of my mouth, ma'am. A

hoot." Jett wondered what his old Ivy League professors and current Fortune 500 business colleagues would think of that assessment. He extended his hand to the young man. "Good getup. You had me going for a second."

"Thank you. Thank you very much." Elvis shook Jett's hand but turned to his sister and cocked one eyebrow knowingly.

"Don't you even go there with me, Elvis Arnold Jenkins!" she said. "I know for a fact that you've earned your way through college by doing your summer gigs. I also know that while you're very good at doing Elvis, you'd make an even better lawyer."

"A lawyer?" Jett eyed the man again.

"Yep." Starla Mae nodded. "He'd make a fine one too; his pre-law professors all say so. And he's been accepted into a fine school, to start next fall—"

"But law school costs money," Elvis said directly to Starla Mae. "Impersonating Elvis in summer hot spots up and down Route 66—that *earns* money. I'm afraid I'm going to have to do a lot more of the latter before I can even hope to begin the former."

"See? Don't he talk like a lawyer already?" Starla Mae's eyes sparkled with pride. "Trouble is, as part-owner of this diner—our folks left it to both of us—he didn't qualify for any financial aid. And we can't convince anyone in charge that this diner isn't capable of supporting itself *and* a law student. Elvis won't take a loan—"

"Honey, we've lived most of our lives in debt. I'm not adding to it. When I've set back enough money, I'll go to law school."

Starla Mae looked at him, her heart in her eyes. She didn't say a word. But Jett got the distinct idea that if she did, it would be about taking risks in order to better one-self and warning against putting off dreams for too long. He imagined she had once given Georgia Darling, in Georgia's high school and college days as a waitress in this very place, the same kind of advice.

The reminder of Georgia made Jett's throat constrict, which put an edge to his tone as he shifted on the counter stool and said, "If it's your dream to become a lawyer, son, you ought to follow it. It might not be as impossible as you think—"

Elvis eyed him warily. "I don't think I caught your name, mister."

"Oh! This is…" Starla Mae extended her hand, palm up, toward Jett. "Well, toss me off the rooftop and call me flighty, but I don't believe I ever got your name either."

"Jett," he said, smiling, despite himself, at her interesting way of putting things. "Jett Murphy."

"Jett," Elvis said. "Jett Murphy. I like that name; I like it very much."

"It's a…it's a nickname," Jett felt compelled to add. "My given name is Padgett."

"Well, welcome to our diner, Mr. Padgett—Jett—Murphy." Starla Mae finally succeeded in latching on to his hand and giving it a firm shake. "'Least it's still 'our diner' for a little while yet, before the bank comes and takes it over, that is. Are you ready to order now?"

"I thought you said nobody comes to this place and 'just orders'?" He sounded a bit more testy than he felt.

"They don't. Or that's how the saying goes," she replied.

"Ah, 'the saying.'" He narrowed his eyes at her.

"You've heard it?" She cocked her head.

He *had* heard this "famous" saying—from Georgia Darling. In fact, he had probably taken it more to heart than he wanted to admit. Still, somehow he felt driven to hear it from the scarlet lips of Starla Mae Jenkins herself. "I have. Why don't you tell it to me, though, just to make sure I've got it right."

"That I can do." She popped a bubble, grinned, and gave him a wink. "'Anyone cruising Route 66 who has lost their love or lost their way will eventually find themselves at the Double Heart Diner.'"

"Hmmm. That's just a bit different than I learned it." Jett narrowed his eyes. "So tell me, do you mean 'find themselves' as in find their way or find their love, or 'find themselves' as in just end up here?"

Starla Mae blew a bubble and shrugged her shoulders.

Something in the kitchen sizzled.

Jett bowed his head and snorted out a humorless laugh. "Guess it doesn't matter. Especially since I have lost my love and I sure enough did end up right here. Guess that proves the saying true."

"Unless you take it the other way," Elvis muttered.

"What?" Jett brushed his fingertips over his faded jeans.

"He means, if you take it that you find yourself—as in find what you're searching for—then you haven't proven the saying right. Not yet." Starla Mae plopped her chin in her hand.

"Not yet, indeed. But if you knew how badly I've messed things up, you'd settle for the looser interpretation," Jett told her. "I don't see how I could ever fix this—or find the love I lost—here tonight."

"What's the matter?" Starla Mae cocked her head, her chin still resting in her palm. "Don't you have any faith?"

"In what? A saying? In a peculiar roadside diner on old

Route 66?" He shook his head. "My faith is in something else entirely." Only God could help him now, though goodness knows he didn't deserve it.

"Then all the more reason never to give up," she said quietly.

Jett held her gaze, fighting the urge to get up, drive back the way he came, and forget everything that had happened these last few days—forget that pretty little redheaded Georgia Darling, who had turned his world upside down, then walked out on him. But this waitress's one solemn statement had him fixed in his seat. If he had faith, he could not simply give up. He had come here to finish something, and even though she didn't know it, that something would be every bit as beneficial to Starla Mae and her diner as it would be to him.

"Why don't you tell us about it?" Starla Mae finally suggested after several seconds of silence.

"Why?" he asked dully.

"Why not?" she answered.

"Well, you've got me there." He laughed, though he was not particularly amused with himself. "I did pray about coming here and felt led to do it. It only seems fitting, after everything I've been through this week, that I'd end up telling my sad story to a waitress named Starla Mae Jenkins and the ghost of Elvis—"

"*Young* Elvis."

Jett nodded to the man in black, conceding, "*Young* Elvis—would-be lawyer—in a place called the Double Heart Diner."

#2 *All That Glitters:* Cindy Reilly launches a hilarious self-improvement campaign to win the heart of her chosen prince. Thanks to an eccentric "fairy godmother" and a disagreeably snooty stepmother, her campaign works—but not the way she'd planned!

Book #3 *A Perfect Stranger:* A beautiful woman is through with romance—until a mysterious pen pal unexpectedly trips up her heart. Then she discovers her sweet, sensitive mystery man is her miserable, undependable, utterly beastly ex-husband—and he wants her back! Available Spring 2000.

Annie Jones
The Route 66 Series:
Meet some incredible characters along historic Route 66—who'll steal more than your heart!

#1 *The Double Heart Diner:* Georgia Darling's mission seemed simple: Save the Double Heart Diner. But things have become more complicated since sophisticated Jett entered the picture. She likes him, maybe too much, but it's clear she can't trust him. Can she save the diner—and her own heart—before it's too late?

#2 *Cupid's Corner:* The feisty lady mayor of a small Kansas city on a stretch of forgotten Route 66 is trying to reestablish its title of Hitchin' City USA by staging a summer wed-a-thon. Will the mayor and the editor of the local newspaper find themselves with their own irresistible itch to get hitched?

#3 *Lost Romance Ranch:* Built by a brokenhearted cowpoke years ago, the once famous dude ranch is now the subject of legal wrangling. When a separated couple is sent off on a treasure hunt along Route 66 to see who will win ownership of the land, can they find the love they've lost along the way? Available June 2000.